Bonjour Alice

Judi Curtin

Illustrations: Woody Fox

THE O'BRIEN PRESS
DUBLIN

First published 2008 by The O'Brien Press Ltd,
12 Terenure Road East, Rathgar, Dublin 6, Ireland.
Tel: +353 1 4923333; Fax: +353 1 4922777
E-mail: books@obrien.ie
Website: www.obrien.ie
Reprinted 2008, 2009, 2011, 2013.
This edition first published 2015 by The O'Brien Press Ltd.

ISBN: 978-1-84717-689-9

13578642
15 17 19 20 18 16

Falkirk Council	
LB	
Askews & Holts	
JF JF	£6.99

Cover design: Nicola Colton
Illustrations: Woody Fox
Layout and design: The O'Brien Press Ltd.
Printed and bound by CPI Group (UK) Ltd, Croydon, CR0 4YY
The paper used in this book is produced using pulp

The O'Brien Press receives financial assistance from

For Dan, Annie, Ellen and Brian.

Many thanks to all my family and friends, who continue to be enthusiastic and supportive, even though the novelty of me being a writer must have worn off years ago.

Everyone at The O'Brien Press has been great as usual, but extra thanks have to go to my editor, Helen, and to Brenda who 'minds' me when I go on tour.

Thanks to Woody for yet more really funny drawings.

Thanks to Sarah Webb who is unfailingly generous with advice for her fellow writers.

Thanks to the many children I've met in the past year, who have shared their great ideas about books and writing. Special mention has to go to the children of Gaelscoil na Ríthe in Dunshaughlin, who kindly invited me to open their wonderful new library – *go raibh maith agaibh*.

Chapter One

I was sitting in front of a giant-sized bowl of green stuff – cabbage, broccoli, spinach and, worst of all, brussels sprouts. Alice's mum, Veronica was standing beside me, shaking her long, sharp fingernails near my face.

'Eat every single scrap,' she said. 'Or else I'm taking Alice back to live in Dublin, and we're never coming back to Limerick. Ever.'

Then Veronica gave an evil laugh, and ran out of the room, slamming the door behind her.

Tears began to roll down my face, dripping into the bowl of vegetables, making them even soggier and more revolting than they had been before.

How could she do this to me?

How could anyone treat a child like this?

Surely there are laws against this kind of thing?

Suddenly Mum was beside me. She patted my arm and smiled.

'Don't mind Veronica,' she said. 'She's just cross because she broke a fingernail. You don't have to eat all this stuff.'

As she spoke she took the bowl and scraped every scrap of food into the bin. Then she put another bowl in front of me.

'Here, love,' she said. 'Try this instead.'

I gasped. This bowl was piled high with every kind of sweet I could imagine. It was like something that had come out of Willy Wonka's chocolate factory. There were sparkling jellies, white chocolate bars, swirly lollipops, and lots, lots more.

'Go on, Megan,' Mum encouraged me. 'Eat up, it'll do you good.'

I reached into the bowl and took out a bar of white chocolate. I ripped off the wrapper and shoved the chocolate into my mouth. Mmmmm. The chocolate began to melt on my tongue, and my mouth was filled with sweetness. I was reaching for a long pink and purple jelly snake, when I felt my arm being shaken.

'Wake up, Megan, wake up. It's your birthday, and you don't want to waste the whole day in bed, do you?'

I rubbed my eyes, and then opened them slowly. Mum was standing next to my bed, smiling.

'Happy birthday, teenager,' she said.

'Thanks, Mum,' I said sleepily.

Mum held out a parcel, all wrapped up in paper that I'd seen on at least three birthdays already. Mum believes wrapping paper should go on for ever.

'Here, Megan,' she said. 'This is from Dad and Rosie and me.'

I took the parcel. It didn't feel like a mobile phone – the one thing I wanted more than anything. Still, I wasn't really surprised. If Mum and Dad gave me a mobile phone, I'd know for sure that I was still dreaming.

Just then my little sister Rosie appeared at my bedside.

'Happy birthday,' she said. 'Can I open your present for you?'

I smiled at her.

'How about if we do it together?'

Rosie nodded happily and before I could move, she proceeded to rip every scrap of paper off my present.

'Thanks, Mum,' I said.

I tried to smile like this was the best present I'd ever got, but that was kind of hard. Rosie was holding up what looked like about a hundred metres of knitting, in revolting, hairy, brown wool.

'It's a scarf,' Mum said helpfully.

I tried again to smile. A scarf? Who would ever wear a scarf that colour? Or that length? And anyway, it was August.

'I know it's August,' said Mum, as if she could read my mind. 'But I had the scarf finished, and I couldn't wait to give it to you.'

I closed my eyes for a second. Maybe I was still asleep. Maybe this was just part of my nightmare.

It wasn't though. Rosie jumped on to my bed, and I could feel her hard knees pressing into my stomach as she tried to wrap the revolting scarf around my neck.

'It's a pretty scarf,' she said, making me wonder if Mum had ever taken her to have her eyesight checked.

Mum sat down on the bed beside me.

'That's only part of your present,' she said. 'After breakfast, the three of us are going to town, and I'll buy you something new to wear. How does that sound?'

That sounded just perfect.

'Thanks, Mum,' I said, meaning it this time. 'I'll get up now.'

Mum didn't move though. She had that dreamy look on her face that meant she was going back in time again.

'My little girl a teenager already. I can't believe it. I remember this day thirteen years ago. It feels like it was only yesterday. The doctors wanted to give me drugs, but I said no. "I'm having this baby naturally," I said. And then—'

I put up my hand.

'Please, Mum. Stop,' I said. 'Don't say any more. It's much too much information.'

Mum smiled.

'Sorry,' she said. 'I suppose I was getting carried away. I just wish I could make you see what a special day it was for your dad and me. Anyway, get up, and I'll make you some porridge for breakfast.'

'But it's my birthday,' I wailed.

'So it is,' she smiled. 'I'll make you an extra-big bowl.'

Then she and Rosie went out of the room.

I lay in bed for another few minutes. I could see through the curtains that it was a beautiful sunny day. It was the holidays. It was my birthday and at last I was a teenager. Surely things couldn't be any better?

Then I saw the revolting brown scarf curled up on the end of my bed, like a hairy, brown snake. I had to smile to myself. If only my mum made delicious chocolates for a hobby instead of knitting gross stuff, then my life would be totally perfect.

Chapter Two

After I'd finished a dangerously huge bowl of porridge, I stood up to clear off the table. Mum pushed me gently aside.

'It's your birthday,' she said. 'You don't have to help.'

I grinned at her and almost dropped the bowl I'd been holding. Why couldn't it be my birthday every day?

'Can I call over for Alice?' I asked.

Mum nodded, and before she could say anything else I raced out the back door.

Alice (who is my very best friend in the whole world) gave me a huge hug when she opened her front door.

'Happy birthday,' she said. 'It's nice to have you here with me. It was lonely being a teenager all on my own.'

'Ha, ha,' I said. 'Very funny. Not.'

Alice always gives me a hard time, just because she's a few days older than me. I pretend not to mind, but secretly I wish I could be the older one.

Alice dragged me upstairs.

'Come on,' she said. 'I have your present.'

I allowed myself to get excited. Alice always buys great presents. We got into her room, and Alice handed me a tiny package. It was wrapped in never-before-used pink paper, and narrow white ribbons. I gasped. It was almost too beautiful to open. I carefully untied the ribbons, and peeled back the paper. Inside was a tiny white box. I opened the box to reveal a layer of fluffy white cotton wool. I lifted the cotton wool to discover a cute silver flower on a chain. Engraved on the flower was 'Megan'. I picked it up to look a bit closer.

'Turn it over,' instructed Alice.

I did as she said, and saw that on the back it said 'My best friend'.

I smiled. The necklace was so beautiful I didn't know what to say. 'Thanks' was the only word I could think of, so I said that, and then gave Alice a huge hug. I hoped that was enough to let her know just how happy I was.

Finally she struggled free and went to sit on her bed.

'Did your parents get you something nice?' she asked.

I hesitated. I didn't want to be disloyal to Mum and Dad, but how could I pretend to like the revolting scarf?

'Er ......' I began.

Alice grinned.

'Is it so nice that you can't begin to describe it?'

I grinned back at her. She knew my parents well enough to know the kind of thing they were likely to give me for my birthday.

'Something like that,' I said. 'But Mum's taking me to town later, and she's going to buy me something new to wear. Do you want to come with us to help me choose?'

Alice sighed.

'I'd love to,' she said. 'But Dad says if my room isn't tidied by lunch-time, he's going to flush my phone down the toilet.'

I laughed. Alice's dad is great at making up punishments that are never going to happen.

* * *

Later, Mum brought Rosie and me to town, like she'd promised. Luckily the summer sales were on, and even Mum couldn't complain that everything was 'outrageously expensive'. In the first shop, I tried on a great short skirt and a spaghetti top, and a hoodie. I stood in the changing room and admired myself. I thought I looked great, and I delayed going out to show Mum, because I knew exactly what she would say.

'Hurry up,' called Mum eventually. 'Come out and show us how you look.'

I pulled back the curtain.

Mum smiled.

'That's a lovely skirt,' she said. 'But where's the rest of it?'

'Is some lost?' asked Rosie.

I smiled at her.

'No, Rosie,' I said. 'The skirt is all there. That's just Mum's idea of a joke. She means she thinks it's too short.'

I turned to Mum.

'I *so* love this outfit,' I said. 'Can I get it? Please, please, please, please, please?'

And to my total surprise, Mum said,

'Well, in my opinion it's a bit short. But you're thirteen now, and I suppose you know what you like. You can get it if that's what you want.'

I gave her a huge hug, and didn't even pull back when her frizzy hair scraped the side of my face. Maybe she was turning into the mother of my dreams after all.

*   *   *

After lunch, Alice came over, with our other friends, Grace and Louise. We hung out for a while, and then we watched a DVD on Grace's fancy new portable DVD player.

The day before, I had begged Mum to let us order a pizza for my birthday tea, but she said no. (And I had to put up with a huge long lecture about how bad it would be for us.) Instead she promised to make us 'a delicious home-made pizza with organic toppings'.

The girls were really nice about it, and no-one laughed as they were picking funny-looking green things out of their pizza. And no-one complained when they nearly broke their teeth on Mum's very chewy home-made pizza dough. And when they were going home, everyone said they'd had a really good time and I think they even meant it.

It had been a good day.

Chapter Three

Next morning I sighed when I woke up. It was always like this on the day after my birthday. I felt kind of empty and disappointed because it wasn't my special day any more. I stayed in bed for ages, reading one of the books Louise had given me for my birthday. I could hear Rosie playing in the kitchen, talking to Sunny, the teddy I brought back from Dublin for her at Hallowe'en.

After a while, I could hear Mum on the phone in the hall. She was on the phone for ages, which was very unusual, as Mum does not believe in having long phone conversations. I wondered what was so important, but couldn't find out, as Mum was too far away for me to hear what she was saying.

When I was half way through my book, I got up. Mum was off the phone at last. She was in the kitchen, tidying up. I stood in the doorway, watching her. She was kind of skipping around, and singing as she worked – very strange, even for her.

'Hi, Mum,' I said.

'Hi, Megan,' she said, in a funny sing-song voice.

'What's going on?' I asked. 'Are you planning to enter the next series of *The X-Factor*?'

She actually laughed.

'No, I'm not,' she said.

'Then why are you singing?'

She stopped scrubbing the sink and turned to face me.

'Because I'm happy, that's why.'

I sighed. The last time I'd seen Mum this happy, she was planning a trip with a bunch of crazy hippies to a music festival in Galway. That had all ended in tears when her sister Linda came to mind Rosie and me, and ended up in the middle of one of Alice's crazy plans to get her parents back together.

'Er ......' I said. 'Why exactly are you so happy?'

Mum beamed at me.

'Because we are all going on a trip, that's why.'

I gulped. I *so* did not want to go on one of her crazy trips. Mum's idea of a fun day out was a day cleaning a park, or gathering litter from the banks of a river.

'You can ask Alice to come with us, if you like.'

I shook my head.

'Thanks, but no thanks. Alice actually has a life.'

Mum made a face when I said that, but she didn't say anything. I felt a bit guilty, so I smiled at her.

'Where are we going anyway?'

Mum beamed again.

'Well, Lucy, my friend from the organic gardening club, has a summer house, and she's always saying that we can borrow it whenever we want, because she hardly ever goes there. And this morning I suddenly decided we could all do with a bit of a break, so I rang Lucy, and she said the house is empty at the moment. She says we can have it for ten days.'

I still wasn't very interested. Knowing Mum's friends, the house was probably a falling-down shack in the middle of nowhere. Mum seemed to be waiting for something else though. I decided to be nice to her. After all, she had bought me that lovely new outfit the day before.

'Where is Lucy's house?' I asked.

Mum spoke lightly.

'Oh, nowhere very special. Just a little village in France.'

I wasn't sure I'd heard right.

'France?' I repeated. 'The house is in France? Like France across the water, next to Germany and all those other foreign countries?'

Mum laughed.

'Yes. That's the one.'

'And we're going there?'

Mum laughed again.

'Looks like it. I've already phoned the travel agents. We got a late booking on the ferry, and it's a special offer because of a cancellation. So it's all booked. We're going on Monday.'

This was so totally amazing. I'd never been abroad before. I raced across the kitchen, and hugged Mum for ages. She laughed.

'My second hug in two days. You'd better be careful or I'll start getting used to it.'

Suddenly I remembered something.

'What did you say about Alice?' I said.

Mum smiled.

'Yes, I said Alice can come with us. The price on the ferry is for the car and five passengers, so it won't even cost any extra, and there's plenty of room in the house. That's if you think she'd like to come.'

I put my head down.

'Sorry about that thing I said earlier,' I said. 'I didn't really mean it.'

Mum patted my shoulder.

'That's OK,' she said. 'You could both bring your bikes if you like.'

I smiled. I could suddenly picture Alice and me cycling down a French lane in the sunshine, chatting and laughing over nothing. This was going to be *so* much fun.

'Do you think her parents will allow her to come?' I said suddenly.

Mum nodded.

'I phoned her dad before you got up. He said it's fine with him, if Alice wants to go.'

'So she knows already?'

Mum shook her head.

'Probably not. Peter was at work and he was

on his way to a meeting. He said he'll talk to Alice at lunch-time. So if you get there before that, you can be the one to tell her.'

I grinned. I *love* telling good news.

Mum smiled too.

'Now sit down and have some breakfast, and then you can go over to Alice's and see if she'd like to come with us,' she said.

I think I must have created a world record for fast porridge-eating, then I leapt up from the table and raced out to call for Alice.

Chapter Four

I rang Alice's doorbell for ages. How dare she be out, when I so badly wanted to tell her the good news?

Then I remembered that she'd spent the night at her mum's apartment around the corner. I raced around there, and when I reached the front door I was so breathless I could hardly talk.

'Alice,' I puffed into the intercom. 'Can I ...

come in? I have to ... talk to you.'

Alice buzzed me in, and I went up to her apartment. She opened the door, and I followed her to her bedroom. It was totally trashed.

'I know,' she said, when she saw me looking around. 'If I don't have it tidy by lunch-time, Mum's banning me from TV for a week. Trust me, it's no fun having two bedrooms to keep clean.'

I sat on the beanbag in the corner, and Alice sat on top of a heap of clothes on her bed. I was so excited, I didn't know how to start.

'I have some great news,' I said finally.

Alice grinned at me.

'So have I.'

I felt a bit disappointed.

'Oh,' I said. 'Well, you tell first then.'

'No, you,' said Alice.

'No, you,' I insisted. Surely my good news was going to be the best, so it was better to save that until last.

'OK,' said Alice. 'Grace rang last night, and invited me to go to stay with her family in their villa in Lanzarote.'

I could feel a sudden pain in my tummy.

'When?' I asked.

'Next week,' replied Alice quickly. 'Her dad's got an extra week off work, so they've just decided to go.'

The pain in my tummy got worse. How could this happen? France would be so much more fun if Alice was there. Suddenly the idea of being with just Mum and Dad and Rosie seemed kind of boring. And to make things worse, Alice would be over in Lanzarote having fun with Grace.

'But what about Louise?' I blurted out. 'Why didn't Grace ask Louise to go with her? They're supposed to be best friends.'

'Grace *did* ask her, but Louise couldn't go. She's bridesmaid at her cousin's wedding, remember?'

And what about me? I felt like asking. Why hadn't Grace asked me to go with her? She didn't know that I was going to France. And I'd been friends with her before Alice had. I'd been friends with Grace ages ago, when Alice was still living in Dublin.

Then I could feel stupid tears stinging the back of my eyes. I blinked hard and looked at Alice.

'Could you tell Grace you can't go with her?' I said quietly.

Alice shook her head.

'Why would I want to do that? It's going to be *so* great. Grace's house is on a big estate. They have their own swimming pool. It's even got a slide. And there's crazy-golf. And they have these totally cool motor-scooter things they're allowed to use for going around the grounds.'

Suddenly I felt like a total idiot. What good were stupid old bikes in France, when you could be on a motor-scooter in Lanzarote? And there was no chance of Mum's friend's house having a swimming-pool. Knowing the kind of people Mum hangs out with, we'd be lucky to have a bath. And instead of crazy-golf, all I had were two crazy parents.

I blinked again and tried to smile.

'I suppose you won't be saying no then,' I said.

Alice gave me a strange look.

'No. I won't be saying no. Anyway, I've already told Grace I'll go with her. And Mum says it's OK. It's all arranged.'

So that was that. My holiday was ruined before it had started. Why had Mum ever suggested that Alice come on holidays with us? If she'd never mentioned it, I wouldn't feel so bad now.

I stood up.

'I need to go home,' I said. 'I have to help Mum with ...... Well, I just have to help Mum.'

'But what about *your* great news?' asked Alice. 'You never told me your great news.'

I shook my head.

'It doesn't matter. It wasn't such great news really. And like I said, I have to go home now.'

Alice came over and stood next to me.

'Tell me your news before you go. Please.'

I shook my head again. I *so* didn't want to talk about France. I *so* wanted to go home and lie on my bed and scream and cry and punch my pillow.

Alice put her hand on my shoulder.

'I'm sorry Grace asked me and not you,' she said. 'She probably only asked me because she felt sorry for me, because my parents don't live together any more.'

It was nice of Alice to say that, but it didn't help very much.

'I really have to go,' I said, and I pushed past Alice and ran down the stairs.

'OK,' she said. 'I'll call for you later.'

Don't bother, I felt like saying, but I couldn't because I was already crying too much.

Chapter Five

I didn't feel like talking, so I let myself in the back door, hoping to sneak past Mum. No chance – she's like a guard dog, who reacts instantly to every creak of every door in the house.

Suddenly she was in front of me. When she saw that I was crying she came over and gave me a long hug. It was nice – all warm and comforting. But it didn't change anything. It didn't change one single thing.

I sobbed until Mum's dress was all soggy.

Then Rosie came in from the garden.

'Why is Megan crying?' she asked. 'Did she fall down and hurt herself?'

'Don't worry, love,' Mum said. 'Megan's fine.'

'So why is she crying?' repeated Rosie.

'She just is,' said Mum. 'Now why don't you go in to the other room and do a jig-saw?'

'Jig-saws are boring,' said Rosie.

Mum sighed.

'Well go and watch TV or something.'

I could hear Rosie doing little skips of joy.

'Yay, TV,' she sang. Then she skipped off into the other room.

Mum squeezed me tight, and then she gently pushed me away from her and we both sat at the kitchen table.

'Do you want to tell me what's wrong?' she said softly.

'Alice can't come to France,' I said.

'But her dad said—'

I interrupted her.

'Her dad was wrong.'

Mum stroked my hair.

'Oh, I'm sorry, love. I know you must be very disappointed.'

I nodded. How could I begin to explain how disappointed I was?

'You could ask someone else to come with us,' said Mum. 'What about Louise, or Grace? They're both nice girls.'

'But they can't come,' I protested. 'Louise has to go to a wedding, and Grace ...' I had to stop to wipe away more tears, before I continued. 'Last night Grace invited Alice to go to Lanzarote with her, and Alice said yes, and that's why she can't come to France with us.'

I stopped talking and put my head in my hands. Mum edged closer and cuddled me.

'Oh, darling, I'm so sorry,' she said. 'That must make you feel worse, knowing that Alice will be with Grace.'

I nodded. Maybe I was being selfish, but that

did make the whole thing much worse.

Mum patted my arm.

'But don't worry,' she said. 'You and I and Dad and Rosie will still enjoy ourselves. France is a beautiful country, and we'll have a wonderful time there.'

I nodded. What else could I do? I didn't want to hurt her feelings, and besides, crying wouldn't change anything. Alice was going on holidays with Grace, and nothing I could do would change that.

I stood up and tried to smile.

'Thanks Mum,' I said. 'I think I'll go down to my room and see what clothes to bring to France.'

Mum gave me one more hug.

'OK, love. That's the spirit.'

Then I went down to my room, lay on my bed and cried some more.

Chapter Six

A bit later I heard the door-bell ring. I didn't bother getting up to see who was there. Probably just one of Mum's boring friends.

Then after another while there was a tap on my bedroom door. I jumped up and rubbed my eyes. Then I opened a drawer and threw a few t-shirts on to my bed.

'What do you want, Mum?'I asked. 'I'm busy sorting out my clothes.'

'I'm not your mum.' It was Alice's voice. For once in my life, I wasn't very happy to hear her. I needed more time on my own.

'You'd better come in,' I said.

Alice came in and sat on my bed. She was grinning like crazy. I figured she was probably thinking about all the cool stuff she and Grace were going to do in Lanzarote.

'Are you packing for France?' she said.

'So you've heard?'

She nodded.

'Yes. I've heard. We are going to have *so* much fun on holidays together.'

I looked at her carefully.

'You mean you and Grace?'

She punched me on the arm.

'No, Dork-head. Not me and Grace. Me and you.'

'But ... but ... but ...'

Alice punched me on the arm again.

'Do you know any other words besides "but"?'

'But …'

Alice laughed.

'Ok, you just be quiet and I'll explain everything. You see, not long after you left my house, Dad phoned and told me that your mum had invited me to go to France with you.'

'And …'

'Oh, I'm glad to see that you do know another word,' laughed Alice. 'And, I told Dad about the Lanzarote trip. And then we didn't know what to do. So Dad phoned Mum and they had a long chat. And then Mum phoned Grace's mum and explained the situation. And Grace's mum was really nice, and she said they hadn't confirmed the tickets yet. So now Grace has invited a friend from her riding school to go with her, and I'm going with you. So everyone is happy.'

'But …'

Alice laughed.

'I'm not going on holidays with you unless you learn a few new words.'

I laughed too.

'But what about the swimming pool, and the crazy-golf, and the motor-scooters? Wouldn't you prefer to be in Lanzarote?'

Alice shook her head.

'You're my best friend. I'd prefer to be with you. And besides, Grace is really nice, but her family is very posh. I know I'll have more fun with you.'

'Are you sure?'

Alice nodded.

'Sure I'm sure.'

All of a sudden everything seemed wonderful again. I was thinking how great the trip was going to be, when Alice interrupted my happy thoughts.

'Know what?' she said.

'What?'

'If Mum and Dad were still living together, we wouldn't have had all that confusion about Dad saying one thing and Mum saying another.'

'And?'

'Well, I've been thinking, and I've come up with this really cool plan to get Mum and Dad back together.'

I couldn't *believe* what I was hearing. Alice had spent most of the year plotting and scheming to get her parents back together. She'd got herself (and sometimes me) into loads of trouble, and nothing had changed – her parents were still separated. But after Easter, after yet another plan had failed disastrously, Alice had promised me that she was finished with plotting and scheming. She told me that she knew her parents were never getting back together. And even better, she said that she was cool with that. And I had believed her.

Alice looked thoughtful.

'This plan will work, I promise, Megan. I'll just need your help.'

So what else was new?

I turned away from Alice and looked out of

the window. I needed to think. What could I say that would make Alice see sense? How could I find the right words?

Suddenly I heard a strange sound behind me. I turned around and saw Alice rolling around on my bed, laughing like she was going to die.

'Gotcha,' she said. 'Had you worried, didn't I?'

I didn't reply.

'Sorry, Meg,' she said. 'I couldn't resist. But I was joking. I told you ages ago I was finished with plotting to get Mum and Dad back together, and I meant it. I was just winding you up.'

For one second, I was really cross, and then I saw the funny side of it. I grabbed a pillow, and whacked Alice with it. She grabbed another, and whacked me back. The pillow burst open, and for one second I thought we could have a really cool fight like they do in movies, with feathers flying everywhere. No chance though – Mum believes in loopy allergy-free pillow-fillings so

Alice and I were showered with a cascade of gross orange-coloured lumps of foam.

'Oops,' said Alice. 'Let's clear all this up, and then I can help you pack ... for our trip to France!'

I gave her one more whack with my pillow, and then I hugged her.

This was going to be the best holiday ever.

Chapter Seven

Next day, Alice and I walked down to the shop to buy some broccoli for Mum. We were talking about all the cool things we were going to do in France. Then, as we turned the last corner, Alice grabbed my arm.

'Stop,' she hissed.

I did as she told me.

'What is it?' I asked in a scared voice. 'Is it that

horrible dog that snapped at Jamie last week?'

'No,' said Alice. 'It's worse. I just saw Louise and Grace going in to the shop.'

'And the problem is?'

'I don't want to meet Grace. I'm a bit embarrassed about first saying I'd go on holidays with her, and then changing my mind.'

That kind of made sense. And now that I thought about it, I wasn't sure I wanted to meet Grace either. After all, she had invited Alice to go with her to Lanzarote even though I was friends with her first.

We stood on the footpath trying to make up our minds.

'We could just go home and tell your mum there was no broccoli in the shop,' suggested Alice.

I nearly always do what Alice suggests, but this time I wasn't so sure that she was right. Suddenly I made a decision. I shook my head.

'No, that's stupid. They're our friends. We

should go and talk to them.'

Alice looked surprised for a second. Then she said, 'You're right. That was a stupid thing to suggest. Let's go and meet them.'

When we got to the door of the shop, Grace and Louise were on the way out. They looked surprised to see us. We all said 'hi' and then we stood looking at each other. Alice looked embarrassed, Grace looked embarrassed, Louise looked puzzled, and I didn't know what to say.

Eventually Louise spoke.

'Grace and I are going to my house. I'm going to show her my bridesmaid's dress. Do you want to come?'

Alice and I looked at each other. Then I made the decision for both of us.

'We'd love to,' I said. 'I just have to buy something for Mum, and drop it home, so she won't call the search and rescue teams. Then we'll go over to your place. OK?'

'OK,' said Louise, and then she and Grace set

off for home.

*　*　*

Twenty minutes later, Alice and I arrived at Louise's place. Louise let us in.

'Alice, will you help me get some drinks?' she said. 'Meg, why don't you go up to my room? Grace is there.'

I didn't have much choice, so I did what I was told, and went upstairs. Grace was sitting on Louise's bed. She went kind of red when she saw me. I could feel my face going red too.

'Hi,' she said.

'Hi,' I said back.

Then no-one said anything for ages. Grace fiddled with an old doll of Louise's, and I played with the necklace Alice had given me for my birthday. I wished Louise and Alice would hurry up, and bring the drinks.

Suddenly Grace spoke.

'I'm sorry I didn't invite you to come to Lanzarote with me.'

'That's OK,' I said, even though it wasn't.

'I wanted to ask you,' said Grace. 'I wanted to ask both you and Alice, but Dad said there was only room for one extra, because my brother is bringing two friends. And then I couldn't decide which one of you to ask. So Mum said I should choose Alice, because she'd had such a hard year with her parents splitting up and everything.'

So Alice had been right about that.

'I'm really sorry,' repeated Grace.

'That's OK,' I said, and this time I meant it. 'Alice is a bit embarrassed too,' I said. 'Because she's coming with me, and not you.'

Grace smiled. 'It doesn't matter. I've invited Saffron, a girl from my riding school. She's really nice, so I know we'll have a great time. And next summer, my brother is going to Irish college, so Mum says I can bring three friends to Lanzarote. I hope you and Alice and Louise will all be able to come.'

Just then Louise came in carrying a tray of

cold drinks. Alice was following her, holding a huge bowl of crisps. Alice put the crisps down on the table, then she went and hugged Grace.

'I'm sorry I won't be going to Lanzarote with you,' she said. 'I hope you have a great time.'

Grace smiled at her.

'That's OK,' she said. 'And I hope you and Megan have a great time in France.'

'What about me?' wailed Louise. 'I'm not going anywhere.'

I grinned.

'But you're going to be a bridesmaid. I've always wanted to be a bridesmaid.'

'Oh yes,' said Louise. 'I nearly forgot, with all this talk of holidays. Will I get my dress and show you?'

The rest of us nodded happily.

'It's in my mum's bedroom,' said Louise. 'Will I put it on?'

We all nodded again, and Louise went out of the room.

'Louise seems very happy,' said Grace.

'Yes,' agreed Alice. 'Her dress must be gorgeous.'

A minute later, Louise was back.

'What do you think?' she asked, as she twirled around.

Grace, Alice and I looked, and looked. Then we looked some more.

'Isn't this the coolest dress you've ever seen?' asked Louise.

Those weren't exactly the words I'd have chosen. I'd have said something like *that is the most gross, disgusting, revolting, horrible piece of clothing I've ever seen in my whole life.* (And trust me, with a mother like mine, I've had plenty of chances to see gross clothes.) The dress was bright, bright pink and shiny. It came almost down to the ground, and it had huge, puffy sleeves. On the neck, there was a ribbon almost the size of Louise's head. Poor Louise, how was she supposed to go out in public looking like that?

'Well,' said Louise. 'What do you all think?'

'Er, it's a very pretty colour,' said Grace.

Alice reached out and touched the dress.

'The material is lovely and soft,' she said.

'It's ... it's ... well ... it's perfect for a summer wedding,' I muttered, repeating something I'd heard my mum say once.

Louise turned away from us all, and put her head down. I sighed. She knew the dress was gross, and we hadn't lied very successfully. I racked my brain, trying to think of something suitable to say, when Louise suddenly turned around again.

'You're all big, fat liars,' she said, laughing loudly. That was true, but why did Louise seem to find it so funny?

'You should see your faces,' said Louise. 'I wish I'd had a camera. Thanks for trying to be kind though.'

'What's going on?' asked Alice.

Louise laughed again.

'My cousin brought this dress over last week, and said it was the one she'd chosen for me to wear as her bridesmaid. She made me try it on right away. And I was *so* totally embarrassed. I thought I'd die. I thought I'd have to invent some deadly disease, just so I wouldn't have to wear it. But it was only a joke. This is just an old dress that used to belong to my cousin's mother.'

We all laughed than. It had been a good trick to play.

Louise ran to the door.

'I'll try on the real one now,' she said.

Minutes later she was back.

'Now what do you think?' she asked.

'Er ...' said Alice.

'Em ...' said Grace.

'Well ...' I said.

Louise looked like she was going to cry.

'Don't you like it?' she asked.

We all laughed.

'Just getting you back,' said Grace.

'It's totally beautiful,' I said, and I meant it.

So Louise did a few twirls in her totally beautiful bridesmaid's dress, then she changed again, and we hung out for the rest of the day.

Chapter Eight

Bright and early the next Monday morning, Alice and I were sitting on my front garden wall, trying not to laugh. It looked like everything we owned was spread out on the driveway. There were boxes and bags and cases and deckchairs. Rosie was already sitting in the car, excited about our big trip.

Dad was trying to pack everything into the car-boot, but every time it looked like he was nearly finished, Mum came rushing out of the house carrying something else.

She handed him a big cardboard box. Dad staggered under the weight of it.

'What's in here?' he asked. 'The kitchen sink?'

'Very funny,' said Mum. 'It's just ...' she mumbled the end of the sentence, so no-one could understand her.

'It's just what?' asked Dad.

Mum spoke quietly,

'It's just a few cans of organic chick-peas.'

Dad dropped the box to the ground, narrowly missing Mum's toes.

'You've got to be joking,' he said.

'I'm not, actually,' said Mum. 'We might not be able to buy these in France, so I thought it best to bring a few cans.'

Now Dad laughed, but he didn't sound very happy.

'Sheila, we are going to the food capital of the world,' he said. 'I don't think we need to burden ourselves with the entire contents of our local health food store.'

Mum put on a sulky face.

'All right so, I'll bring them back into the kitchen.'

Dad smiled.

'Thanks, love,' he said. Then he turned back to the boot, and, while he wasn't looking, Mum sneaked three cans of chick-peas under Rosie's car-seat and a few more on the floor in the back of the car. Then she winked at Alice and me.

'Lucky Dad didn't see me packing the cans of lentil stew earlier on,' she said.

Then she took the rest of the cans back in to the house.

Alice giggled.

'Your parents are so funny,' she said.

I sighed.

'I hope you'll still think that after ten days on holidays with them.'

Just then Mum came out of the house carrying a box of washing powder.

'Megan,' she hissed. 'Distract Dad.'

I shook my head. I wasn't getting involved.

Alice was though.

'Hey, Donal,' she called.

'Will there be enough room for my roller-blades?'

Dad looked up, but Mum wasn't quick enough. Dad raced over and grabbed the box of washing powder from her, and held it in front of him like a shield.

'No way,' he said. 'No way is that coming. Either it stays here, or I do.'

Mum pretended to think.

'OK, so,' she said slowly. 'The washing powder can stay here.'

Then they both laughed.

'What were you planning to do with it?' Dad said. 'Were you planning to take in washing in France?'

Mum shook her head.

'No, but who knows if I'll be able to buy

environmentally-friendly powder in France? I didn't want to take any chances.'

Dad grinned at her.

'What are you like?' he said. 'How about if you put a small bit of the powder into a bag or something, would that do?'

Mum nodded.

'I suppose so.'

Then they had a big sloppy kiss. I covered my eyes.

'Stop that. It's gross,' I said.

I looked at Alice. She looked kind of sad. Then I felt really stupid. Poor Alice would probably love to see her parents kissing like that.

Suddenly Alice made a face.

'Here come Mum and Jamie. I'm glad I said good-bye to Dad before he left for work this morning.'

I looked up to see Veronica wobbling along the footpath in very, very high heels. She was wearing a beautiful light blue dress, much fancier than the outfit my mum wore for my confirmation. Jamie was walking beside her, wailing,

'I want to go to France. Why can't I go to France?'

'If you're a good boy, I'll take you to the cinema. Will that do?' said Veronica.

'Yay, cinema,' screeched Jamie. 'That's *much* better than France!'

Alice and I laughed.

Veronica reached us, and said hello to everyone.

Mum gave her a big hug, and I could see by Veronica's face that she wasn't very happy about that. She was nice, though, and tried to smile.

'Now I don't want you to worry, Veronica,' said Mum. 'We'll take good care of Alice. I'll make sure that she eats plenty of fresh fruit and vegetables. We'll aim for seven portions a day, just to be on the safe side.'

'Oh, thanks, Sheila,' replied Veronica, but I could see by her face that she wasn't really too worried about how many portions of fruit and vegetables Alice ate over the next ten days.

Veronica hugged Alice.

'Be a good girl,' she said.

Alice grinned at her.

'Am I ever anything else?' she asked.

Her mum kissed her on the cheek.

'Well, let's not discuss that now, shall we?' she said and everyone laughed.

Five minutes later, the house was locked up, the car was packed and Alice and I had strapped our bikes securely onto the bike-rack on the back of the car.

'All set?' said Dad.

Everyone nodded except for Rosie who'd been in the car for so long that she had fallen asleep.

Then the rest of us jumped into the car, waved madly at Veronica and Jamie, and set off to catch the ferry to France.

Chapter Nine

A few hours later, a man in a yellow jacket was directing us on to the biggest ship I had ever seen.

'Be careful, Donal,' said Mum, over and over again. 'Drive slowly.'

'I'm driving slowly,' said Dad. 'Any slower and I'd be stopped.'

I made a face at Alice, but she just laughed.

At last the car was parked, and we were able to get out. Everyone had packed a small bag with just enough stuff for the night on the boat. We all got our bags and Dad locked the car. Then we had to climb a big long stairs until we got to the deck where the cabins were.

There were hundreds of cabins, and it took ages to find ours. Mum had booked two – one for Alice and me, and the other for Mum, Dad and Rosie. Ours was the cutest little room ever – about the size of a small cupboard. There was just a set of bunkbeds, and a tiny room with a toilet and a shower.

'Do you want the top bunk, or will I have it?' asked Alice.

I shrugged. I really didn't care. I was just happy to be there, to be on holidays with Alice for ten whole days. (And I was also happy that Mum and Dad hadn't done anything too embarrassing yet.)

Then we all raced up on deck to wave goodbye to Ireland. We stood on the deck, until Ireland was only a small grey line, far away. Mum sighed.

'Aaaah. To think we won't see our home for ten days.'

I shook her arm.

'That's a good thing, isn't it,' I said.

Mum didn't answer. She can be very strange sometimes.

Alice and I were allowed half an hour to explore then, before we were to meet the others again for tea. The ship was *huge* – so big that we kept getting lost. Not counting the decks where the cars were parked, there were six other decks. Some just had cabins, but the others had shops and restaurants and bars. Alice stopped outside one restaurant, and looked at the menu, which was displayed in a fancy glass case.

'This all looks totally yummy,' she said. 'And I'm starving. Which restaurant do you think we'll be eating in? One of my friends from Dublin went on a ferry once. She said the kiddies meal was just sweets and crisps and a fizzy drink. Are we too old for kiddies meals, do you think? After all, we *are* thirteen now.'

I sighed. Didn't Alice know what my parents

were like? There was zero chance of us having a meal consisting of nice stuff.

Unfortunately I was right. We went to meet Mum and Dad and Rosie, and my heart sank when I saw that Mum was carrying a huge picnic bag.

'Sorry, Al,' I said. 'Looks like there's not going to be any kiddies meal for us today.'

Alice shrugged.

'Who cares? Anyway, I love picnics.'

I tried to smile. That's only because she'd never had one of Mum's specials before.

Dad didn't look very happy either.

'Er, Sheila, love. Why aren't we eating in a restaurant?'

Mum shook her head.

'I doubt if they'd have organic food like the stuff I've brought. And besides, I'd say the food is very expensive in those restaurants. Bringing our own is a good way of saving money.'

Dad sighed.

'Maybe we should have swum to France altogether,' he said. 'That would have saved us a fortune.'

Mum hit his arm playfully, and then she led the way to a big table by the window, and began to spread out the food. First there was brown bread that might once have been in slices, but now looked more like brown breadcrumbs.

'Oh, dear,' said Mum when she saw the state of it. 'Luckily I brought plates.'

Everyone was given a plastic plate, and Mum piled a heap of breadcrumbs onto each.

'Don't worry,' said Mum. 'I've got lots of tasty toppings.'

Then she pulled out lots of small plastic containers, and opened each one with a flourish, like it was gold or jewels or something. Then she listed the names,

'Houmous, pesto, olives, guacamole, fig relish, organic lettuce.'

It was like a kids' nightmare. Where were the

sausages, the ketchup, the cheddar cheese?

I could feel my face going red. I was used to this kind of stuff, but what about Alice? She hardly ever ate meals in my house, and now I thought I could see why. It had been stupid to ask her to come with us. She was going to hate every second. I turned around to her, ready to whisper an apology, when she beamed at me.

'Yum,' she said. 'All my favourites. Thanks Sheila.'

She must have been lying, but I wasn't quite sure.

'You're welcome, Alice,' she said. 'It's nice to see a girl with healthy tastes. And for afters, there's a choice.'

I crossed my fingers behind my back. *Please don't think it's something nice like cake, or ice-cream* I said to myself.

Alice kept smiling.

'I hope it's some nice fresh fruit,' she said.

Mum beamed at her.

'You're in luck,' she said. 'I've got some apples, some bananas, and a lovely dish of fresh green grapes.'

Alice was still smiling.

'Looks like it's my lucky day,' she said.

Mum turned around to help Rosie to stick some breadcrumbs together with a piece of houmous.

I leaned close to Alice.

'What are you on?' I asked. 'Mum's never going to fall for it if you keep going on like that.'

'Like what?' asked Alice innocently.

'Like all that stuff is your favourite food.'

'OK, so it's not exactly my favourite,' said Alice. 'But it's OK. And it was nice of your mum to go to so much trouble. My mum would never do that. She'd just buy us pizza.'

'And the problem would be?'

Alice laughed.

'Even pizza gets boring after a while.'

I sighed.

'I'd love the chance to find out.'

Alice sighed too.

'I wish my mum would cook a bit more.'

I laughed.

'I hope you get your wish,' I said. 'And don't worry, the first thirteen years are the hardest.'

'What are you girls whispering about?' said Mum. 'Eat up. There's lots more where this came from.'

'Yum, yum,' said Alice, and we all laughed.

Chapter Ten

After we'd eaten our delicious meal (not), Mum and Dad decided to take Rosie to watch a magic show.

'Can Alice and I go off on our own,' I asked.

To my surprise, Mum nodded.

'Sure. Just be back at the cabin in an hour.'

'We will. I promise,' I said, as we raced off before she had time to change her mind.

Alice and I had great fun for a while. At first we pretended we were film stars, rehearsing for a remake of *Titanic*. Then, when we were tired of that, we sneaked up to an outside deck and pretended we were explorers, visiting oceans that had never been visited before.

A bit later, I was pretending to be a super-model, on my way to a fashion shoot in New York. I was walking my best walk along a corridor, saying,

'... now we have Megan, wearing the latest design from Paris, she—'

Suddenly Alice grabbed my arm.

'Stop,' she said. 'You've got to stop right now.'

I jumped.

'What is it,' I said. 'What's wrong?'

'I've just seen the worst thing ever.'

'Is it my mum with another picnic basket?' I said.

Alice giggled.

'No. But be serious, Megan. It really is the worst thing ever. Look down there.'

I followed where she was pointing and gasped in horror.

'But it can't be,' I said.

Alice didn't reply.

'It couldn't be,' I said. 'It just couldn't be.'

Alice sighed a big, long sigh.

'If it walks like Melissa, and flicks its hair like Melissa, and has the exact outfit Melissa was wearing last time I saw her ... then it probably is Melissa.'

The person-who-probably-was-Melissa, was walking along with her back to us. I could see an iPod in her hand. Suddenly I heard the familiar, false, tinkly laugh. Alice and I looked at each other.

'It's Melissa,' we said together.

'Run,' I said. 'Before she sees us.'

'Great idea,' said Alice, but before we could take a single step, Melissa gave one huge flick of her hair, and turned to face us.

She seemed shocked at first, and then she arranged her face into kind of a smile. Alice and I said nothing as she walked towards us.

'Alice, Megan,' she said when she got close enough. 'What a surprise. Of all the boats in the world, imagine us all showing up on this one.'

I remembered that Alice and I had promised not to hate Melissa any more, so I tried to smile.

'We're really surprised too,' I muttered.

Melissa gave me one of her most false smiles.

'I can't believe you're going to France on your holidays,' she said. 'I really didn't think that was your kind of thing.'

I didn't answer. I was still a bit surprised to be going to France myself.

Melissa continued.

'What hotel are you staying in? We're going to a super-cool one. It's got three swimming pools. And five restaurants.'

I put my head down. What would Melissa say if she knew that instead of eating in fancy restaurants, we'd be dining on cans of food that Mum had brought all the way from Limerick?

Alice came to the rescue as usual.

'We're not going to a hotel,' she said. 'We're staying in a hundred-year-old *"gateau"*.'

I tried to catch her eye, but she babbled on without noticing me.

'It's a really fancy *gateau*. It's got—'

Just then Melissa's crazy Goth sister came up and started to talk to her. I grabbed Alice's arm, and pulled her to one side.

'What are you on?' I hissed.

'I don't know what you mean,' she protested. 'I couldn't listen to any more of her going on about the fancy hotel, so I made up that stuff about the *gateau*.'

'But you do know what *"gateau"* means?' I said.

For the first time, Alice looked doubtful.

'It means castle, doesn't it?'

I shook my head, laughing.

'Sorry, you should have paid more attention when Mum was trying to teach us those words during the car journey. *"Chateau"* is the French word for castle.'

.

'Oops,' laughed Alice. 'Then what does "*gateau*" mean?'

I started to giggle.

'It means cake.'

Now Alice started to giggle too.

'So I just told Melissa that we're staying in a hundred-year-old cake?'

I nodded.

'But it doesn't matter. Melissa didn't say anything, so obviously she didn't see your mistake.'

'Maybe she was just being polite?'

I laughed again.

'Melissa? Polite? I don't think so. Obviously she has no idea what a *gateau* is, but she'll never admit it.'

Just then, Melissa's sister went away, and Melissa gave us all her attention again.

'So, where were we?' she said.

Alice looked at her with a serious expression on her face.

'I was just telling you about the beautiful *gateau*

we're staying in. All the best people stay in *gateaus*. I can't believe you've never stayed in one before.'

I smiled to myself. Melissa is a terrible snob, and she would die rather than admit that she hadn't done something that all 'the best' people did.

She flicked her hair over her shoulder.

'Oh, she said. 'I've stayed in loads of *gateaus*. Last year we stayed in a huge one. It was one of the finest *gateaus* in France, according to my dad. It was ...'

She stopped talking and put on a superior face.

'What are you two laughing at?'

Alice and I were practically rolling around the ground we were laughing so much by now.

Melissa tossed her head.

'Really,' she said. 'I'd have thought that now you're nearly in secondary school, you might be starting to get a bit mature.'

Alice put on a scared face.

'Mature?' she said. 'Not mature. Anything but that.'

And then we laughed some more.

Eventually we recovered, but we couldn't shake Melissa off. I suppose she had no-one else to hang out with, except for her crazy sister.

At last I looked at my watch.

'Alice and I have to go now,' I said. Melissa looked disappointed, and for a second I actually felt sorry for her.

Then she said.

'Did Mumsy say you had to get back for early beddy-bye-byes?'

I very quickly stopped feeling sorry for her. We said our goodbyes, and began to walk away.

Suddenly Melissa called, and Alice and I stopped and looked back at her.

'Maybe I'll see you tomorrow at breakfast?'

Alice made a face.

'Not if we see you first,' she whispered. And

then we skipped off to our cabin.

Chapter Eleven

I didn't sleep very much that night. Alice and I chatted for ages, and then, when we agreed to try to get some sleep, I lay awake for ages, listening to the dull drone of the ship's engines. It was kind of cosy, lying there in our tiny cabin. Alice and I had agreed that I could have the top bunk this time, and that she could have it on the way home. Our cabin was so small that I could lean over and see out through the tiny round window. Most of the time, all I could see was the sea, which looked black, and kind of scary. Once though, I saw a small far-away boat, looking very lonely in the dark night.

I awoke to hear Mum beating on the cabin door.

'Get up, girls,' she was calling. 'We're nearly there. Time for breakfast.'

I sat up, groaning. It felt like I'd just fallen asleep. I looked out through the port-hole, and saw land in the distance.

'Look. Look,' I said excitedly to Alice. 'Look out there. It's France.'

Alice rolled over and rubbed her eyes.

'What did you expect?' she asked. 'Japan?'

I leaned down from my bunk, and tried to hit her with my pillow, but missed.

'Very funny. Not,' I said. 'It's easy for you to be all cool. It's different for me. I've never been abroad before.'

Alice sat up.

'Sorry. I *am* excited. It's just that I'm tired too, and at the moment, the tired part of me is winning.'

We both got up, and dressed quickly.

'I'm starving,' said Alice, when we were ready. 'Do you smell rashers and sausages?'

I sighed.

'Yes, I do smell rashers and sausages. It must be coming from the restaurant. But don't get too excited. I bet Mum has other plans for us. Sorry.'

Suddenly I had a horrible thought. Was I going to spend the entire holiday apologising to Alice for my mum's crazy ways? Was Alice already sorry that she wasn't on holidays with Grace and her family?

Alice just grinned happily.

'I don't care what your mother's plans are,' she said. 'As long as they involve food. I'm so hungry I could eat a—'

'—a houmous sandwich?' I finished for her.

Alice laughed.

'Yes. Even that.'

We went next-door to Mum and Dad's cabin. Rosie was so excited, she couldn't sit still.

'We're nearly there. We're nearly there,' she kept saying, jumping up and looking out the tiny window.

Dad smiled at Alice and me.

'Good girls,' he said. 'I'm glad you're ready. We only have fifteen minutes before we have to get to our car.'

'We'd better hurry on up to the restaurant,' I said hopefully.

'Restaurant indeed,' said Mum. 'Do you think we're made of money?'

Suddenly I felt both cross and embarrassed.

'No,' I said quickly. 'I know you're not made of money. I bet you're made of stupid, disgusting, organic porridge.'

'Megan!' said Dad in his crossest voice.

'Ignore her,' said Mum. 'She's just trying to impress Alice.'

Impress Alice? I thought. *If I really wanted to impress Alice, I'd have left her at home, far away from my mad mother and her revolting food.*

Suddenly I felt sorry. It was really nice of Mum and Dad to let me bring Alice on holidays with us. And if Alice wasn't complaining about the food, why should I? After all, I'd had thirteen years to get used to it.

'Sorry, Mum,' I said quietly.

'That's OK,' she said. 'I forgive you. Now, be a good girl and pass me the flask of porridge.'

I gulped. She had to be joking. Didn't she? Even Mum wouldn't travel around Europe with a flask of porridge in her luggage.

Just then Mum burst out laughing.

'I'm joking,' she said. 'And it was worth it to see your face. We're not having porridge. I've brought a lovely bag of muesli, with extra nuts and seeds, and Dad got a carton of milk in the restaurant, so we're all sorted.'

I tried to smile. After the thought of porridge that was nearly a day old, muesli actually sounded nice.

We ate quickly, and then packed up and got

ready to go back to our car. On our way to the car deck, we passed Melissa and her family. I couldn't help glancing at Mum, who looked her usual messy self. I got ready for Melissa to say something nasty. Melissa surprised me though. She smiled, and said,

'Bye, Megan. Bye Alice. I hope you have a really nice time at your *gateau*.'

Alice and I grinned.

'I hope you have a nice time in your hotel,' I said.

When they were gone, I turned to Alice.

'It would be easier to hate Melissa, if she didn't sometimes surprise me and actually sound nice.'

'Well,' said Alice. 'Don't worry too much about it. In September she'll be far away in her fancy boarding school, and we'll probably never see her again.'

I tried to feel sad about that, but couldn't manage it.

'Hurry up, girls,' said Dad then. 'If we don't

get a move on the boat will turn around and go back to Ireland with us still on board.'

There was *no way* we were going to let that happen. So we all hurried up and minutes later we were packed up in our car, ready for our holiday to begin properly.

Chapter Twelve

It took two hours to drive to the village where our cottage was.

Then we spent an hour driving around in circles looking for the right cottage.

We started on what looked like the main street. Mum's friend had given her an old, crumpled envelope with directions written on it. Mum read aloud.

'Turn left at the shop,' she said.

Dad sighed.

'I know it's not exactly Paris, but there are quite a few shops here. Which one do you think she means?'

Mum turned over the envelope,

'Oh, there's more writing here. "Bread, butter, brussels sprouts" ... oh no, I think that must be Lucy's shopping list. Sorry, Donal, I don't know which shop she means.'

'Could we phone her and ask her?' asked Dad.

Mum shook her head.

'Sorry. She's gone on a meditation course for two weeks – no phones allowed.'

Dad gave an even bigger sigh.

'Now why doesn't that surprise me?' he asked. 'That means we'll have to try every turn, until we find the right one.'

He drove past the first shop, and turned left. Mum kept reading from the envelope.

'Take the next right, then turn left on to the first lane you see. The house should be at the end of the lane.'

Dad did as he was told, and stopped the car when we came to the first lane on the left. It was very narrow and overgrown.

'What do you think?' he said.

'Could be right,' muttered Mum.

So Dad drove down the lane. It went on for miles and miles. Just when we were about to give up, we turned one last corner. Dad stopped the car again.

'Wow,' he said.

'Wow,' said Alice.

'Wow,' said Rosie.

'No way,' I said.

We were in front of a huge, white house. It looked like it had about a hundred rooms, and in front of it was a huge swimming pool.

Mum sighed.

'Sorry guys,' she said. 'This time I have to agree with Megan. I don't think this could be Lucy's place.'

'Should we go in and check?' asked Dad

hopefully.

Just then a man came out of the house, and walked towards us shouting loudly in French.

'Er ... *Bon ... jour* ...' said Dad.

Mum opened her window.

'Lucy?' she said.

The man kept shouting.

'Lucy?' said Mum again, louder this time.

The man shouted even louder.

Dad turned around to us.

'Don't you two girls speak any French?' he asked.

I shook my head. And even if I did speak French, I wasn't sure I'd fancy practising it on this crazy Frenchman.

'I know two French words,' said Alice helpfully. 'I can say "cake" and "castle" in French.'

'Thanks,' said Dad. 'But I don't think either of those words is what we need right now.'

'Well, I only know about ten words of French,' said Mum. 'But even I can understand that this does not appear to be Lucy's place. Turn the car around, Donal, and let's get out of here.'

Dad did as he was told, and we drove away. I looked back to see the cross Frenchman waving his fist and still shouting.

We went back to the main street, and tried turning at another shop. This time we ended up driving right into a farm-yard. Ducks and chickens clucked around the car.

'Oh, listen,' said Alice. 'The birds speak the same language as the birds at home.'

Just then, two dogs ran out of a barn.

'Nice doggies,' said Rosie, before they bared their teeth and started snarling like they wanted to kill us.

Dad didn't wait to be told – he revved up the engine, and backed out of the farm-yard at top-speed.

Our third attempt led us to a tumbling-down cottage at the end of the narrowest lane we'd been on yet. There were no dogs, or shouting men, so we all got out of the car and stood in front of the house. If this was our holiday home, I *so* did not want to be on holidays.

'What do you think, Sheila?' asked Dad. 'Is this it?'

'Don't be ridiculous,' said Mum. 'I think Lucy would have mentioned it if her house didn't actually have a roof.'

We all climbed back into the car. We were getting tired, and this really wasn't much fun any more.

'Right,' said Dad. 'This has gone beyond a joke. We'll try one more time, and if we don't find it, we're checking in to the nearest hotel for the night.'

'Yay!' Alice and I said.

'Over my dead body,' Mum said.

So we drove back to the main street, turned at the baker's shop, turned right, and then left on to a small lane. This time we ended up outside a tiny stone house. It had a sweet little red door, and there were climbing plants all around it. It was like a house from a fairy story book. And even better there wasn't a dog, or a shouting man in sight.

'What do you think?' asked Dad, for what felt like the fiftieth time that morning.

'One way to find out,' replied Mum.

She fished in her handbag for the key Lucy had given her, and then she jumped out of the car. She went up to the front door, turned the key, and to our great delight, the door swung open.

'Yay!' we all shouted happily, as we tumbled out of the car.

Mum stood at the door of the house,

'Welcome to your holidays,' she said, as we all ran past her to explore.

Chapter Thirteen

That evening was *so* much fun. Alice and I picked a tiny attic bedroom, and we spent ages putting all our clothes into a cute little wardrobe. Then, when everyone was unpacked, Dad drove us to the beach nearby, and we swam for ages, and didn't even turn blue.

On the way back, we drove to the supermarket, and Mum got so excited by the display of organic chicken, she forgot all about the cans of lentil stew, and the chick peas, so we had an almost normal dinner. When we were finished, Alice sat back and sighed.

'That's the nicest dinner I've ever eaten,' she said, and I think she really meant it. Then Mum beamed at her, and Dad hugged Mum, and Rosie hugged Alice, and it looked like maybe this was going to be a fantastic holiday.

Alice and I talked for ages before we went to sleep, so we slept very late in the morning. When we woke up, we could hear Mum downstairs, clattering around in the kitchen.

'Donal,' she called. 'I can't find the porridge. I know I packed two bags, and I can't find them anywhere. Have you seen them?'

'No,' said Dad.

Then Mum raised her voice.

'Girls, are you awake? And did either of you unpack the porridge?'

Alice suddenly started to laugh.

'Why are you laughing?' I asked. 'Since when is porridge so funny?'

Alice giggled again.

'I'm the one who unpacked the porridge.'

'And? That's funny because?'

'Well, let's just say I did some advance unpacking.'

'What on earth are you on about?' I asked.

Alice sat up in bed.

'I unpacked the porridge before we left Limerick. I sneaked it out of the car, and hid it in your garage when none of you was looking.'

Now I laughed too.

'I didn't know you hated porridge that much,' I said.

Alice shrugged.

'I don't. I quite like it actually – especially with honey on top. But I know how much you hate it, so I thought I'd do you a favour.'

I gave a big, happy smile.

'Now that was a big favour. Thanks, Al.'

'Girls,' called Mum suddenly, and her voice was much closer than before. Suddenly she opened our bedroom door. 'Good morning. And did you hear me calling? I was wondering if one of you unpacked the porridge.'

I looked at Alice, and Alice looked at me.

'Sorry, Mum,' I said. 'Neither Alice nor I has seen one flake of porridge since we arrived in France.'

It wasn't a lie, but it wasn't really what Mum wanted to know.

Alice smiled at her.

'Why don't Megan and I get dressed real quick, and we can cycle down to the baker's shop and buy some lovely fresh bread for breakfast?'

Mum didn't seem able to make up her mind.

'But I was hoping to make some porridge for us all ... oh, I suppose it doesn't matter. We're in France so we'd better do as the French do.'

Five minutes later, Alice and I were cycling to the baker's shop, and it was just like I'd pictured our holidays – all warm and happy and fun.

And the very best thing was, the bread was so nice, Mum didn't mention porridge once more for the entire holiday.

Chapter Fourteen

Next morning, Alice and I offered to go to the baker's shop again.

'I am having *so* much fun,' she said, as we cycled down the lane.

'So you're not sorry you didn't go to Lanzarote?'

'No way. This place is really cool,' she said.

We got to the main street, and propped our

bikes up against a garden wall while we went in to the baker's shop. We came back out, and Alice held the bikes, while I clipped the baguette onto the back of mine. Suddenly Alice grabbed my arm.

'In the garden ...... don't look now,' she hissed.

'Oh no,' I groaned. 'Don't tell me it's Melissa. I thought she was safe in her super-cool hotel with three swimming pools and five restaurants.'

Alice laughed.

'OK, I won't tell you it's Melissa, because it isn't.'

I relaxed and began to turn around.

'I told you not to look,' hissed Alice again.

I grinned.

'OK, I won't look. But what am I meant to be not looking at?'

'It's a boy,' said Alice.

'Oh, a boy,' I said. 'That sounds exciting.'

'Be like that,' said Alice. 'But it's not just any boy. It's the best-looking boy you've ever seen.'

'Mum doesn't let me out much,' I said. 'So I haven't seen many boys. And besides, I haven't seen this one yet either.'

Suddenly Alice went all soppy and dreamy.

'OK, so I'll describe him for you. He's ... he's tall ... or at least I think he is, he's sitting down, so it's kind of hard to tell. And he's got lovely dark brown hair, but the ends are blonde, and it's *so* cool. And his eyes, well he's too far away for me to see them properly, but I bet they're gorgeous. And he's wearing this totally cool denim shirt, and he's—'

I interrupted her.

'What exactly is he doing, while you're standing here telling me how gorgeous he is?'

Alice smiled a dreamy smile.

'He's reading a book. I bet it's not one of those stupid war books that the boys in our class read. I bet it's something totally romantic, like Shakespeare. He's—'

Suddenly I realised something.

'If he's reading a book, then he's not looking this way, is he? So that means I can look at him.'

As I spoke, I turned around, but as I did so, the bikes toppled over, and crashed to the ground with a huge clatter. I ignored the bikes, and looked over the wall into the garden. The boy had jumped to his feet, and Alice was right – he was tall, and he was very, very good-looking.

Now though, he was also looking this way, probably wondering why two embarrassed look-ing Irish girls were peering over his garden wall.

Alice smiled.

'Hi … er … that is … I mean … *Bon … jour.*'

The boy didn't smile back at us.

'*Bonjour,*' he said. Then he picked up his book, and went in a door at the back of the baker's shop.

Alice pretended to faint up against the wall.

'Did you hear that?' she said. 'Did you ever hear such a perfect French accent?'

'He *is* French,' I replied.

'I know,' said Alice. 'But that accent, I think it's the sweetest sound I've ever heard.'

'I think the sweetest sound I ever heard was when you told me the porridge was left behind in Ireland,' I said, laughing. But I knew what she meant. That boy, whoever he was, was interesting. Very, very interesting.

'I wonder what his name is?' said Alice dreamily.

'Seamus? Padraig? Rumpelstiltskin?'

Alice punched me on the arm. Obviously she had recovered from her faint, because the punch hurt.

'Stop messing,' she said. 'I bet he has a gorgeous name – maybe Jean, or François—'

'You mean, John, or Francis?'

Alice tried to punch me again, but I was ready for her this time, and she missed.

'Well they sound better in French,' she said.

I sighed.

'Anyway, what does it matter?' I said. 'He's

gone. We're never going to see him again.'

Alice picked up her bike.

'Maybe you're never going to see him again, but I intend to. Tomorrow is another day, and guess who's coming here to buy bread for the breakfast?'

'Us?'

Alice patted my arm this time.

'Clever girl. Got it in one,' she said. 'Now let's go back, before the bread gets cold, and your Mum starts threatening to make porridge.'

Chapter Fifteen

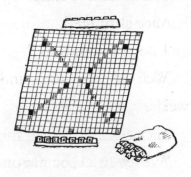

The next morning wasn't much different. Alice and I cycled to the shop, raced in and bought the bread, and then raced back out to see if the boy was in the garden.

Before I even saw him, I knew he was there, because Alice had that dreamy look on her face again, and she was fixing her hair so much that I thought she had turned into Melissa.

I looked past her, and saw the boy sitting exactly where he had been the day before. He was reading again, but he was too far away for me to see what book he had. Today he was wearing a really cool striped shirt, and denim jeans. He looked like a movie star.

'Now what?' I said.

Alice shrugged.

'I don't know, do I?'

'Well we can't just stand here for the day, can we?'

Alice sighed.

'Why not? I'd be happy to stand here forever, just looking at him.'

'Alice O'Rourke, get over yourself,' I said.

'Must I?' she said in a dreamy voice that was starting to annoy me.

Just then the boy looked up from his book, and stared right at us.

'Quick. Say something,' said Alice.

'But he's French. What can I say? I can't ask him what kind of music he likes, or what's his favourite sport. Do you think he'd like to hear me say *gateau* or *chateau*?'

The boy stood up, which made Alice panic.

'He's going. Quickly, Meg, think of some-thing.'

'Er, *bonjour*,' I said.

'He didn't hear you. Say it again.'

So I said it again – a bit louder than I'd intended.

'*BONJOUR.*'

The poor boy actually jumped. Then he said a real quick '*bonjour*', and practically ran into the back of the baker's shop.

Alice sighed.

'I think I'm in love,' she said.

'Hey,' I said. 'What about me? Can I love him too?'

Alice shook her head.

'Sorry, Meg, I saw him first.'

'But that's not fair,' I protested.

Alice laughed.

'No, I suppose it isn't. Anyway, what does it matter? It's not like one of us is going to ever go out with him or anything. We've got six more days — that's six more "*bonjours*". We can take turns.'

'OK,' I said, climbing on to my bike. 'Now let's go. Last one home gets extra lentil stew for dinner.'

*　　*　　*

Later that day, Mum walked in to the village to buy stuff for dinner. When she came back, she came out to the garden to where Alice and I were lying in the shade of a tree, playing Scrabble.

'I have great news for you two girls,' she said.

'You found the porridge?' said Alice, winking at me.

'Don't be cheeky, young lady,' said Mum, but I could see she wasn't really cross.

'What's the great news?' I asked. I'd known Mum for long enough to know that stuff she thought was great news, usually turned out to be totally boring. Still, Alice was beating me at Scrabble, and I had all vowels, so I was glad of the distraction.

'Well,' said Mum, putting down her shopping bags, and throwing herself on to the grass next to them. 'I got chatting to the lady in the baker's shop – she speaks very good English – and she said that she has a son about your age.'

Alice and I sat up very quickly. This was starting to sound interesting.

Just then an ant crawled onto Mum, and she became absorbed in watching it crawl down her leg. (Mum doesn't believe in shaving her legs, so the poor ant must have thought it was lost in a forest.)

'And?' I said to Mum, trying to remind her that she was supposed to be giving us good news. 'What about the baker's son?'

The ant escaped from the forest, and Mum turned back to us.

'Oh, yes, the baker's son. His name is ... let me see ... what did she say his name was?'

'His name doesn't matter,' said Alice. 'What else did she say about him?'

Mum wasn't giving up though.

'It began with "B". Now what was it again? Bernard? Bertrand? No, it wasn't any of them. Now, let me think ...'

Mum was fiddling with her hair, like she always does when she's trying to think of something. Alice gave me a look that was easy to understand – *can't you make her get on with it?*

I shook my head. We'd get no more information until Mum remembered the boy's name.

'Ben? Bill? Barry? Bonaparte?' I said helpfully.

Mum shook her head. Then she suddenly clapped her hands (always a good sign.)

'Bruno,' she said happily. 'That's it. He's called Bruno.'

Alice gave a sudden giggle.

'My granny used have a dog called Bruno,' she said. 'He could do loads of tricks. He used to go to the shop every morning, and carry the paper all the way home. He—'

'Al,' I said.

'Oh, sorry,' said Alice. 'You were saying, Sheila?'

'Well,' said Mum. 'As I said, Bruno is about your age, and he's learning English at school, and he'd like to practise it.'

I gave a big smile.

'He can practise on us any day.'

'Well, I'm glad to hear you say that,' said Mum. 'These days I'm never quite sure how you're going to react. I was half afraid you'd say you wouldn't want to wander around the village with some French boy.'

Alice smiled.

'Oh, don't worry,' she said. 'Wandering around the village with some French boy is exactly our idea of fun.'

'Well I'm glad to see you're being mature about it, Alice dear,' said Mum. 'Because his mother said she'll send Bruno over tomorrow morning at eleven, and he can show you around the village. Now, I can't stay here chatting, I'd better get started on the dinner.'

She picked up her shopping bags, and went in to the house.

Alice ran her hand across the Scrabble board, sweeping all the letters on to the grass.

'What did you do that for?' I asked, before I remembered that I had all vowels, and was losing the game anyway.

Alice looked at me like I was crazy.

'We don't have *time* for Scrabble,' she said. 'We have much more important things to do now. We've only got ...' She looked at her watch and then continued, 'We've only got eighteen and a half hours to get ready for Bruno.'

Chapter Sixteen

Next morning I woke to hear Mum calling up the stairs.

'Megan, Alice. Get up. Time to go for the bread.'

I started to climb out of bed, but Alice leaned over from her bed, and pulled me back.

'Wait. We can't go to the bakery this morning,' she said.

'Why not?' I asked as I pulled my socks on.

'Duh. Because we'll see Bruno.'

'Duh to you too. Don't we want to see Bruno?'

Alice sat up, and looked at me like I was a total idiot.

'Of course we want to see Bruno, but not yet. We're not ready.'

I was pulling on my t-shirt by now.

'Speak for yourself,' I said. 'I'm nearly ready.'

Alice sighed.

'No, you're not. You're not ready at all. We've got to plan our clothes, and shower, and do our hair, and our nails. We've got to—'

I held up my hand to make her stop.

'We're not going to a ball. We're only going for a walk around the village. We don't have to dress up.'

'Whatever,' said Alice. 'You do what you like. But I've decided that I'm going to make a special effort.'

That settled it. If Alice was going to look all pampered and pretty for Bruno, there was no way I was going to look like a scarecrow. I called down to Mum.

'We're feeling a bit lazy this morning. Could you or Dad go for the bread, please?'

Mum laughed.

'I suppose so. But I hope you'll have the energy for the walk around the village with Bruno.'

Alice giggled.

'Don't worry. We'll have plenty of energy for that.'

After breakfast, Alice and I both showered. As soon as our hair was dry, I tied Alice's up in a bun. Then she did a really cool French plait all down the back of my hair. Alice put on a really nice denim skirt and a blue and white striped t-shirt. I looked in my wardrobe, and wasn't happy with what I saw, but Alice picked out a pair of jeans, and lent me a white shirt to go over them.

'You look lovely,' she said. 'Now just our nails,

and then we're ready.'

'OK,' I said. 'Get out the nail varnish then.'

Alice sighed.

'I didn't bring any. Did you?'

I shook my head.

'Didn't think I'd need it.'

Alice giggled.

'What about your Mum?'

I giggled too.

'I think I heard her say she's just finished her last bottle.'

'We'll just have to keep our hands in our pockets at all times then,' said Alice. 'We can't have Bruno seeing our un-varnished nails.'

I gulped.

Was Alice starting to turn into her mother?

Then Alice poked me in the arm.

'I'm kidding,' she said. 'Now I think we're ready. Let's go.'

We went out to the garden to show Mum and Dad.

Mum looked at us like we were ghosts.

'Girls, you look ...' she said. Then she couldn't say any more.

'I hope this Fido is worth it,' said Dad.

'Behave yourself, Donal,' said Mum. 'You know well that his name isn't Fido.'

'Rover?' said Dad winking at Alice and me.

Mum laughed.

'It's Bruno,' she said. 'As if you didn't know. But I agree with you. I hope he's worth all the trouble you've gone to.'

'Oh he is,' said Alice.

'How do you know?' asked Mum puzzled. 'Have you met him already?'

Alice went red.

'Oh,' she said. 'We don't actually *know* that he's worth it. We just hope that he is. That's what I meant.'

Mum was giving her a strange look, but just then the doorbell rang, saving Alice from further explanation.

No-one moved.

'Are you going to get that, girls?' said Dad.

Alice and I looked at each other.

'You get it,' we both said together.

Still no-one moved towards the door.

'Why don't you both go?' said Mum.

It seemed like the best idea, so Alice and I walked slowly towards the front door. This was the moment we'd been waiting for, but now that it was here, I felt kind of shy. Looking over a wall at our dream date was one thing – standing face to face with him was going to be much harder.

We reached the front door.

'This is it,' whispered Alice, as she reached for the handle and pulled the door open.

We stood there with our mouths open.

Where was the beautiful boy with the dark hair tipped with blonde?

Where was the guy in the totally cool clothes?

And what was this small, pale, boy with almost-shaved hair, and ugly, shiny, yellow shorts doing on our door-step?

There was a very long silence.

Finally Alice spoke.

'What do you want?' she asked, rather rudely I thought.

The boy went very red. Even his neck and his ears turned a strange colour a bit like the curtains in Rosie's bedroom.

'*Je* ... I ... I ... Bruno,' he said. 'I come to demonstrate you the France.'

'Bruno?' said Alice.

'Bruno?' I repeated after her like a crazy parrot.

The boy nodded his still-red head.

'But you can't be,' said Alice.

Now the poor boy looked very puzzled. Even though he clearly wasn't very good at choosing clothes, or barbers, surely he knew his own name.

Suddenly I felt sorry for him.

'Why don't you wait here?' I said. 'While we ...

while we ... while we talk to my mum for a minute.'

Bruno didn't say anything, which was good enough for me. So Alice and I left him on the door-step, and ran off.

'Who on earth is that?' hissed Alice as soon as we were safely in the kitchen, with the door closed behind us.

'He says he's Bruno,' I said.

'But it can't be.'

'But it is.'

'And what about the cool guy in the garden of the bakery?' asked Alice.

I shrugged.

'We made a mistake. That wasn't Bruno. That was someone else who happens to live near the bakery.'

'Not just near the bakery,' hissed Alice. 'We saw him go in there, remember? By the back door.'

I shrugged again.

'So maybe he likes bread. Maybe he's a good customer, so they let him in the back way. Maybe he works there. Maybe ...'

I couldn't think of any more maybes, but it didn't matter anyway. We had no idea where *cute-guy* was, but *dorky-yellow-shorts-guy* was waiting on our door-step.

Just then, Mum came in to the kitchen.

'Where's Bruno?' she asked, looking around like we might have hidden him under the table or something.

'He's out the front,' I said. 'But, er, Mum, maybe this tour of the village wasn't such a good idea, after all.'

'Don't be silly,' Mum said. 'It'll do you both good to get out, see the village, meet the locals.'

'But we can't,' said Alice.

'Why ever not?' asked Mum.

'Because ... because ... because he's a stranger,' said Alice. 'And I'm not allowed to go out with strangers.'

I grinned. Trust Alice to think of the perfect excuse.

Or not.

'That's absolutely ridiculous,' said Mum. 'He's not a stranger. I know his mother. Now off you go, and I'll expect you back for lunch at one.'

'But that's two hours,' I said.

'Oh, do you need more time?' asked Mum. 'We could have lunch later if you like.'

I shook my head.

'No. Two hours is plenty.'

'Sure?' asked Mum.

'We're *very* sure,' said Alice, patting the hair I'd spent ages fixing. 'Now let's go, Megan. We don't want to keep Bruno waiting, do we?'

Chapter Seventeen

When Alice and I got outside, Bruno was sitting on the wall outside our house. He jumped up when he saw us coming, and his face, which seemed to have recovered, went all red again.

'*Bon* ... hello,' he said.

'Hi,' Alice and I said.

Then no-one said anything for ages.

Bruno played with his watch-strap, Alice fiddled with her hair, and I kicked a small pebble around on the dusty footpath. This was going to be *soooo* boring.

At last, Alice spoke.

'Er, Bruno,' she said. 'Do you, by any chance, have a brother?'

Bruno nodded.

'Yes. I have brother. He calls himself Serge.'

Alice grinned at me.

'What does he look like?'

Bruno looked puzzled.

'He look like ... I know not ... he has ... how you say ... blonde hairs.'

Now Alice looked *really* happy.

'Can we get him?' she asked. 'Can we ask him to come on our walk?'

'You want that Serge walk with us?' said Bruno.

Alice nodded.

Bruno gave a big shrug and waved his hands in the air.

'If you want.'

Alice nodded again.

'Yes. We want. Don't we Megan?'

By this time, what I really wanted was to be sitting under the apple tree playing Scrabble, but it was a bit late for that. So I nodded weakly.

'Yes,' I said. 'We want.'

When we got to the bakery, Bruno stopped at the garden wall where Alice and I usually parked our bikes.

'You wait,' he said. 'I get Serge.'

So we waited. Alice was so excited she could hardly stand still.

'We need a plan. How about if you walk with Bruno, and I walk with Serge?' she said.

I poked her in the arm.

'No way,' I said. 'We're all walking together, or else I'm out of here.'

'I was just kidding,' said Alice, but I knew she hadn't been.

After ages, the side door to the bakery opened

again, and Bruno stepped outside. Alice and I both held our breath, and a second later a small, blond boy stepped out into the bright sunshine. He followed Bruno to where we were standing.

Alice couldn't hide her disappointment.

'Where's Serge?' she asked.

'Here,' said Bruno, pointing to the little boy. 'This my brother Serge.'

'But he can't be,' protested Alice.

I had to giggle. Poor Bruno must have thought we were totally crazy. First we thought he didn't know his own name, and now Alice was accusing him of not knowing who his brother was.

Even though I was enjoying seeing Alice so confused, I decided I'd better step in.

'Do you have another brother?' I asked Bruno.

Bruno shook his head, but didn't go red. I suppose he figured there was no point being embarrassed when he was surrounded by two crazy girls.

'Then who ... who was the boy in the garden?

The boy with the book? The *big* boy?'

Suddenly Bruno smiled and pointed to the seat under the tree.

'The boy who always sit himself there? The boy who read all the day?'

Alice nodded enthusiastically.

'Yes, that's him. Who is he?'

'That is my cousin,' said Bruno. 'He calls himself Pascal. He very boring.'

Alice shook her head.

'I bet he's not one bit boring. I bet he's very nice.'

Bruno shook his head.

'No. Pascal is not nice. He spend all the days looking in the mirror. He is very not nice.'

Alice laughed.

'He looks nice to me. Where is he?'

'Gone away,' said Bruno, like he didn't care much anyway.

'Gone away?' repeated Alice like a parrot. 'Is he coming back?'

Bruno nodded slowly.

'Unhappily, yes. Pascal will come back.'

Alice smiled again.

'That's fantastic ... I mean, when is he coming back?'

Bruno thought for a minute.

'Tomorrow.'

Alice beamed so much that I thought her face was going to crack into tiny pieces. Then she gave a totally stupid little dance of happiness.

I smiled at Bruno.

'Don't mind her,' I said. 'She gets like that sometimes.'

Alice glared at me, but I pretended not to notice. It served her right for trying to keep Pascal for herself.

'Come on,' I said. 'Are we going to go on that nice walk? You said you'd like to walk with Serge, didn't you, Alice? I think you two might have a *lot* in common.'

Alice gave me another evil look, but I ignored

that one too, and skipped off down the street.

Chapter Eighteen

I used to think that Alice's little brother Jamie could be a pain – but that was before I met Serge. He was a total monster who made Jamie seem like a little angel. Before we'd gone a hundred metres along the street, I heard a shriek from Alice.

I turned around to see her hopping on one leg, and trying to rub the other leg with her hand.

'The little brat just kicked me,' she said.

I looked at Serge who was smiling sweetly like he'd never done anything wrong in his entire life. I nearly laughed, but changed my mind when I saw Alice's cross face.

'Maybe it was an accident,' I said.

Bruno shook his head.

'I think not accident,' he said so seriously it made me want to laugh again. I put my hand over my face and pretended to cough.

Alice caught up with us.

'If he tries that again I might accidentally slap his cheeky little face,' she said. 'Now, Bruno, what's there to see in this place?'

Poor Bruno went red again. He probably wasn't used to being with someone who is as direct about stuff as Alice is.

'We go see church?' he asked.

I have to admit that visiting churches isn't top of my list of fun things to do on holidays, but it was a tiny village, and if Bruno didn't show us the church, there probably wouldn't be much left to show us. And besides, Alice was looking crosser every second, and I didn't much like the idea of going home and restarting our game of Scrabble. So I smiled my best smile at Bruno, and said.

'Yippee. A church – can't wait to see that.'

Then I grabbed Alice's arm and dragged her after Bruno.

Serge didn't seem very pleased. I suppose visiting churches wasn't his idea of fun either. He ran and pulled Bruno's arm.

'*Bonbons*,' he shouted.

Bruno turned to us.

'It mean sweets,' he said.

Alice smiled at him.

'Now I know three words,' she said. '"*Chateau*", "*gateau*" and "*bonbons*".'

Bruno looked at her like she was a total idiot. By now Serge was throwing a tantrum, screaming loudly in French. Bruno made a face at us.

'Serge a bit ... how you say ...?'

'Spoiled?' I suggested.

Bruno nodded.

'Don't worry,' said Alice, trying to be nice at last. 'You should meet my brother. He's a bit of a pain too.'

She smiled at Bruno and he managed to smile back at her without going too red.

By now we were at the church. Bruno showed us the outside and then the inside. It was just another church, and not exactly the highlight of our holidays so far. As we came back out into the sunshine, Alice pulled out her phone.

'Is that the time?' she said, without even looking at it. 'We ought to go, or your mum will be worried. Bye Bruno.'

Bruno looked surprised that we were going so soon. I knew how he felt. I was a bit surprised too, but as usual, I followed Alice's lead.

'Er, ... bye,' I said.

'Thanks for showing us around,' she said to Bruno. Then she leaned down and whispered to Serge, 'Thanks for nothing, Poo-head.'

I giggled. Luckily Bruno hadn't heard, and Serge didn't understand.

Suddenly Bruno smiled.

'We go more walk tomorrow?' he asked.

I gulped. One walk with this guy was enough for me. How were we going to get out of this without hurting his feelings? Then Alice totally surprised me by saying.

'That would be lovely. See you here at eleven o'clock?'

Bruno just had time to smile before Alice grabbed me and dragged me towards home.

'What's going on?' I asked.

Alice smiled.

'We're going out with Bruno again tomorrow.'

'But why?'

She smiled again, like I was totally brainless.

'Finish this sentence. Bruno is ...?'

I sighed.

'A total dork?'

Alice laughed.

'OK. That too. What else?'

'A fashion disaster?'

'True, but that's not what I was thinking of. Bruno is ... Pascal's cousin. And Pascal is coming back tomorrow. So we go out with Bruno, and we get to meet Pascal. Simple.'

I sighed again. But I knew there was no point in arguing. I knew we'd end up doing what Alice wanted, no matter what I said.

* * *

Mum was surprised when we got back home so early.

'What happened?' she asked. 'Didn't you get on with Bruno?'

Alice smiled at her.

'Oh, we got on just fine,' she said. 'We got on so well that we're meeting him again tomorrow morning.'

Dad looked up from the book he was reading.

'But we're supposed to be going to the hat museum tomorrow.'

Alice managed to look like she really cared.

'Oh dear,' she said. 'What a pity. We've already promised Bruno, so now Meg and I will have to miss the hat museum.'

Dad sighed.

'We could put the hat museum off until the next day.'

Alice shook her head.

'No,' she said. 'We couldn't ask you to do that. You go, and when you get back you can tell us all about it.'

Then we raced out of the room so we could laugh in peace.

Chapter Nineteen

Next morning Alice and I had to spend ages getting ready again, and Dad had to go to the bakery. While he was gone, Mum gave us a big lecture.

'I'm really not very happy about leaving you two girls on your own,' she said.

Alice looked at her innocently.

'You don't have to worry about us, Sheila,' she said. 'You'll only be gone for a few hours, and Meg and I will just be walking around the village with Bruno. We'll be perfectly safe.'

Rosie came over and hugged her.

'I want to go with Alice and Megan,' she said.

Alice looked at me in horror. We were hoping not to have Serge around, and I could see that even a good child like Rosie might get in the way of the romantic morning she was hoping for.

Luckily Mum rescued us.

'No, Rosie,' she said. 'You come with Daddy and me, and if you're good I'll give you an extra rice-cake after lunch. How does that sound?'

Sounded like a bad deal to me, but Rosie smiled.

'Yay! Extra rice cake,' she sang as she skipped out of the room.

Mum turned back to Alice and me.

'I'm still not totally happy,' she said. 'You must promise to be very good.'

'We promise,' said Alice obediently.

Mum smiled at her.

'And don't go making any arrangements for tomorrow, because Dad has something special planned.'

Poor Alice smiled. Didn't she know yet that

anything my mum called special was likely to be totally boring?

Mum continued.

'We're going to the biggest war museum in the region. It's going to be so exciting.'

I sighed. How could a room full of dusty old guns and stuff be exciting? Were my parents ever going to get a life.

* * *

After breakfast, Alice and I set off to meet Bruno.

'Does this feel like when you and Hazel were going on that date with Lee and his friend when we were in summer camp?' I asked.

Alice went red. She hates when I mention Hazel. I know it's because she's still embarrassed over everything that happened.

'No. This is different. Totally different,' she said. 'Anyway, do you think Bruno will wear those gross yellow shorts again?'

I knew she was trying to change the subject,

but I let her away with it.

'Dunno,' I said. 'And why do you care anyway?'

She laughed.

'Because they're the ugliest things I've ever seen? Because even being near them is bad for my image? Because I might just throw up if I have to look at them one more time?'

I had to laugh too. And when we turned around the next corner and saw Bruno standing in the square wearing the yellow shorts, we laughed even more.

He walked towards us.

'You tell a joke?' he asked.

'Sort of,' I said, embarrassed.

'It wasn't very funny though,' said Alice, which made us laugh even more.

Luckily there was no sign of Serge. Unluckily there was no sign of Pascal either.

Alice couldn't wait.

'Where's your cousin?' she asked.

Bruno shrugged.

'He stay with friends' house. He not come back last night.'

Alice and I didn't say anything.

'Is a problem?' asked Bruno.

There definitely was a problem. Didn't the poor guy realise that the only reason Alice and I were there was to see Pascal? I glanced at Alice. She looked like she was ready to tell Bruno the truth.

Before she could say anything, I shook my head so hard it hurt.

'No. There's no problem,' I said quickly. 'Now, what are we doing today?'

'Today I show you war memorial,' said Bruno so proudly that I couldn't say we'd already seen it about fifty times. (It would have been hard to miss it since it was right in the middle of the village.)

Alice and I followed Bruno for the five seconds it took to get to the war memorial. He stood underneath it and pointed.

'The war memorial,' he said, like we were blind and couldn't figure that out for ourselves.

He climbed onto the metal railing and pointed at one name – Bruno Bermond.

'Is my great-uncle,' he said. 'He die when he have only seventeen years.'

I gulped. That was only four years older than me. And for a few minutes, the three of us got kind of sad, standing there in the bright sunshine looking at the names of all the men who had died in horrible wars.

Then Bruno jumped down from the railing.

'Was long time ago,' he said.

We all shuffled around looked at each other for a bit.

'I think it's time we got back,' said Alice suddenly. 'Megan's mum goes crazy if we're late.'

She was right, Mum does go crazy if we're late, but since we were going to be about three hours early, that wasn't likely to be a problem.

Bruno looked disappointed.

'We go walk again tomorrow?' he asked.

Alice smiled at him like she meant it.

'We'd love to,' she said. 'But we can't. We've got to go out with Megan's parents.'

'The day after?' he asked.

'Will Pascal be back then?' asked Alice.

Bruno shrugged.

'I think,' he said.

That was good enough for Alice.

'Then we'll definitely be free to go walking. Eleven o'clock, same place?'

Poor Bruno nodded happily, as Alice and I skipped off towards home.

As soon as it was safe to talk, Alice shrieked.

'Have you *ever* seen anything as gross as those yellow shorts?'

She was right, Bruno's shorts were gross, but maybe that wasn't his fault.

Maybe they were the only shorts he owned?

Maybe they'd been given to him by his ancient granny, and he didn't want to hurt her feelings?

Or maybe yellow shorts were fashionable in France?

Before I could say anything though, Alice giggled.

'Do think he might be wearing them for a bet?' she asked.

It wasn't a nice thing to say, but Alice made it sound so funny, that I couldn't help giggling too. Then I put my arm around her and we laughed all the way home.

Chapter Twenty

The trip to the war museum with Mum and Dad was exactly as I had expected – totally, totally boring.

As we walked past the hundredth glass case stuffed with ancient old documents, Alice whispered in my ear.

'Don't worry, Megan. This time tomorrow we'll be with Pascal, and this whole museum will just be like a bad dream.'

Mum saw her whispering and looked at her with a questioning look.

'Oh,' said Alice. 'I was just saying that visiting this museum is like a dream come true.'

Mum smiled at her, and later I heard her whispering to Dad about what a nice, cultured girl Alice is.

Next morning Alice and I spent ages getting ready again. Once more we giggled all the way in to the village.

Once more Bruno was waiting for us alone, but easy to spot in his bright yellow shorts. I couldn't help feeling sorry for him. Maybe I'd been right. Maybe they were the only shorts he owned. Maybe his family was really poor, and couldn't afford anything else for him to wear.

Alice wasn't in the mood for mocking Bruno's shorts though. She looked like she was going to cry. She almost ran over to Bruno.

'Where's Pascal? Isn't he back yet?' she asked, quite rudely I thought.

'He come back last night.'

'Where is he then?' Alice's voice was even ruder than before.

Poor Bruno backed away from her.

'He have … how you say … a bad head?'

I giggled.

'Do you mean a headache?'

Bruno nodded happily.

'Yes. He have a headache. He rests at home in his bed.'

Alice looked like she wanted to punch Bruno, and Bruno looked like he knew she wanted to punch him.

'It's not Bruno's fault,' I hissed in Alice's ear. 'Now get over yourself.'

Alice gave me a fierce look, and then she gave a small forced laugh.

'Whatever,' she said. 'Now Bruno, what else is there to see in this place?'

'We go to beach?' he suggested, still looking a bit afraid.

I sighed. Alice and I had already been to the beach lots of times. Bruno heard my sigh.

'I know secret way,' he said. 'Is nice way. You follow me.'

'Yippee,' whispered Alice in my ear. 'We get to go on Bruno's secret path. How exciting. Not.'

I giggled, but then felt guilty when I saw Bruno's face. I pulled Alice by the arm.

'Don't be so mean,' I said. 'Now let's go.'

Bruno was right. The secret path through the trees was kind of nice – all cool and mysterious. Bruno walked in front, with Alice and me trailing a long way behind him.

'This is such a waste of time,' said Alice angrily after a while. 'Why are we trekking in this stupid wood behind this nerdy boy who is wearing the grossest shorts in the history of the world?'

'You're just cross because Pascal isn't here,' I said.

Alice stopped and stared at me.

'And you're not?'

I wasn't sure.

Alice had gone on so much about Pascal that he didn't seem like a real boy anymore. He seemed more like a dream, or a film star.

Anyway, if he did show up, I knew he'd like Alice best. I knew she'd be funny and clever, and Pascal wouldn't even notice that I was there.

Bruno was waiting for us at the end of the path.

'This is the beach,' he said, pointing like we hadn't noticed all the sea and sand and stuff.

I kicked off my flip-flops and stepped on to the warm sand.

'We didn't bring our towels,' I said.

Bruno patted his bag.

'Is OK. I have enough.'

He spread three huge towels on the sand, and we all sat down.

We sat there for a while, saying nothing. Suddenly Alice jumped up.

'This is totally boring,' she said, stamping down towards the water.

I was embarrassed.

'I'm sorry,' I said to Bruno. 'She's just in a bad mood. She gets like that sometimes. She'll get over it.'

'Is OK,' said Bruno.

I didn't know what to say. Bruno was being so nice, and that made me feel even more embarrassed. I wanted to get up and go to where Alice was paddling in the water, but I didn't. After all, it wasn't Bruno's fault that he wasn't cool like his cousin.

Bruno reached in to his bag and pulled out a Nintendo DS.

'I have good game,' he said.

He showed me the game, and let me play it, and didn't even laugh when I was totally useless at it. When he was taking his turn, I stood up, planning to call Alice over to play. Then I sat down again quickly. I leaned over to Bruno.

'Isn't that ...?' I began.

Bruno looked up from the game and sighed.

'Is my cousin Pascal,' he said, like this was the worst thing that had ever happened to him.

Pascal walked over and stood beside us. I could hardly believe it.

The moment Alice and I had been waiting for

since forever had finally arrived.

Chapter Twenty-One

A lice had her back to us, and was throwing pebbles into the sea.

'Hey, Al,' I called. 'Come over here.'

She didn't even turn around.

'No. I'm perfectly fine here thanks,' she said sulkily. 'I'm having sooooo much fun in this totally fun place throwing these totally fun stones into the totally fun water.'

I smiled. Sometimes Alice is quite funny when she's cross. (Actually she's always funny when she's cross, just as long as she's not being cross with me.)

'You really should come over,' I called.

Alice threw a big fistful of stones together.

'Just leave me—' she began, turning towards where Bruno and I were sitting, with Pascal standing beside us. Alice's hands fell to her sides, and the last few pebbles plopped into the water. She raced back to us. Suddenly she wasn't cross anymore. She had a kind of sparkly, happy look about her. She held her hand out towards Pascal.

'I'm Alice,' she said with a big smile.

Pascal reached out his hand, then noticing that Alice's hand was all wet and sandy he pulled it back again.

'I Pascal,' he said.

'This is such a beautiful beach,' gushed Alice, as if she'd forgotten that she thought it was so boring just minutes earlier.

Pascal didn't answer.

Bruno stood up.

'This is Megan,' he said to Pascal, pointing at me. He pronounced it 'Meg-anne'.

'Hi,' I said, standing up and holding out my hand.

Even though my hand was perfectly clean, Pascal looked at it like I was asking him to touch a revolting worm or something. Feeling a bit embarrassed, I put my hand into my pocket. I made a face at Alice, but she didn't notice. She was too busy grinning madly at Pascal.

'I love France,' she said. 'I think it's the nicest place I've ever been in my whole life. It's just ... like ... totally cool. And I love the village. I love the war memorial and everything. And the church ... Well ... it's a really cool church. And the house we're staying in ... it's so ... so ... well it's so *French*.'

I felt like laughing. Alice, who's usually so calm, was babbling like she was crazy, in her effort to impress Pascal. It looked like she was wasting her time anyway. He wasn't even listening. He was fixing his hair, and standing there on the sand like being totally cool and handsome was enough.

Suddenly I thought of something.

'Does Pascal speak English?' I whispered to Bruno.

Bruno nodded.

'Yes, but only when he want. Pascal always only do what he want. I tell you before, he not nice boy.'

I was beginning to agree with him, even though Alice was still trying her best to chat to Pascal.

'What kind of music do you like?' she asked.

Pascal shrugged.

'I not like music.'

Alice tried again.

'Films,' she said. 'Everyone likes films. What's your favourite?'

Pascal shrugged again.

'I not like films,' he said.

Alice never knows when to give up.

'What about books?' she said. 'What kind of books do you like to read?'

Once more Pascal shrugged.

'I not like books,' he said.

Now I knew for sure that he was lying. Alice and I had seen him reading in the garden of the bakery lots of times. Alice seemed to have forgotten this. She still wouldn't give up.

'Do you like tennis?' she asked. 'Or soccer? Or rugby? Or anything?'

Pascal replied to each question with a shrug. He'd have very strong shoulder muscles by the end of the day if he went on like this.

Then in the middle of one of Alice's sentences, he put up his hand to stop her.

'Enough,' he said. 'I not want to talk with you anymore. I go home now.'

This was rude enough even for Alice. She

stood there with her mouth open, but no words came out.

Pascal turned to Bruno.

'Good-bye, little cousin,' he said, and then he pushed Bruno so hard that he fell backwards onto the sand. Then he turned and walked away along the beach.

Bruno scrambled to his feet, and dusted the sand off his clothes. His face was bright red.

'Was joke,' he said. 'Pascal make joke with me.'

It hadn't looked much like a joke to me. I turned to Alice to see what she thought. She absolutely *hates* bullies. She always steps in when Melissa picks on anyone at school. Surely she'd do something about what had just happened. But Alice wasn't looking at Bruno and me. She was gazing after Pascal who was already half way across the beach.

I turned to Bruno.

'No offence,' I said. 'But your cousin's a bit ...'

Bruno sighed.

'I know. I tell you many times already. He *not* a nice boy.'

Pascal had gone out of sight, and Alice suddenly remembered that we were there.

'It's not Pascal's fault,' she said. 'He has a pain, remember?'

I giggled.

'He *is* a pain, you mean.'

I turned to Bruno to try to explain.

'When we say some-one is a pain we mean—'

Bruno laughed.

'I understand, I think. You mean he not a nice boy.'

Then we both laughed together. Alice seemed to be in the middle of a sense of humour failure.

'You're *so* immature,' she muttered, and she stamped away and began throwing stones in the water again.

Bruno looked at me.

'She'll get over it,' I said. 'Now give me that Nintendo. I was just getting the hang of that game.'

Chapter Twenty-Two

A while later, I was still playing the Nintendo game, and Alice was still angrily throwing stones into the water. If she didn't stop soon, there was going to be a mountain in the middle of the sea, and the people who make maps would have to draw a new one of this whole area. I'd just been killed in the game, when Bruno took it from my hand.

'I need that I ask you something, Meg-anne,' he said.

'How I got to be so good at this game?' I laughed.

He shook his head.

'No,' he said. 'Is not funny question. Is

important. I need that I ask you something important.'

I looked up and noticed that he'd gone red again. He looked even more nervous than he had the first day we'd met. I gulped. This sounded serious. Was there a crazy kind of rule in this place that if you went walking with a person more than twice, you had to get engaged or something?

I picked up a handful of warm sand and let it slip through my fingers.

'So, is OK? I can ask you this question?' said Bruno.

I nodded. Unless I ran away, there didn't seem to be any way of avoiding his important question.

Bruno took a deep breath.

'Meg-anne, do you ...'

I felt a bit sick. This was going to be *soooooo* embarrassing. I just knew it.

He took another deep breath.

'Do you ... do you ... do you like my short trou-sers?'

I'd thought he was going to ask me something really serious, and all he was interested in was those stupid shorts that Alice and I had been mocking for so long. I couldn't help myself. I started to giggle. Bruno looked hurt.

'Is a joke?' he asked.

I tried to keep a straight face as I shook my head.

'No, it's not a joke.'

'So do you like my short trousers or no?'

'Shorts,' I said as brightly as I could. 'In Eng-lish they're called "shorts". "Short trousers" sounds wrong. It's like saying—'

Bruno interrupted me.

'So do you like my short trousers or no?'

He just wasn't giving up.

Should I lie or should I tell the truth?

If I lied would he believe me?

If I told the truth would he hate me?

I looked around for Alice. She's always good in this kind of situation. But she'd wandered along the beach and was too far away to call.

I took a deep breath.

'Well. They're very ... er ... very ... they're a bit ...'

'You not like,' said Bruno quietly.

Suddenly it didn't seem fair to lie to him. I had to tell the truth.

'I not like ... I mean I don't like them. Sorry, Bruno.'

Bruno smiled.

'Is OK. I not like either.'

I looked at him in surprise.

'If you don't like them, why do you wear them? Every single day?'

He sighed.

'Pascal give me. When my mother tell me to meet you on first day, Pascal, he give me shorts and he tell me they is nice. He tell me Irish girls will like. And I silly boy. I believe him. So I wear shorts every day. Every night I wash so I can wear again.'

Suddenly I felt angry. Pascal knew those shorts were horrible, but he persuaded Bruno to wear them anyway.

He must have known that Alice and I would laugh at them.

He must have laughed when he saw poor Bruno washing them every evening.

What kind of mean bully would do that to his own cousin?

'Pascal is not nice,' I said. 'He's very not nice.'

Bruno smiled sadly.

'I tell you so already. Why you not believe me?'

I smiled back.

'Next time I'll believe you. I promise.'

'Tomorrow we can walk again?'

I nodded. 'Sure. If you want.'

'OK. In the morning I help my father. So you call my house after noon?'

I nodded.

'Sure.'

'And I not wear yellow shorts.'

I laughed.

'OK. We'll call for you after lunch and there won't be a pair of yellow shorts in sight.'

I'm not sure if he understood me, but he laughed anyway.

Then he handed me the Nintendo.

'Is your turn, I think.'

I was really getting the hang of the game when Alice came back and threw herself onto the sand beside us.

'What time is it?' she asked. 'I'm starving. I'm so hungry I could eat a horse. No, even worse, I could eat a whole bowl of lentil stew.'

I giggled. I was glad to see that she'd got over her bad mood.

'It's five to one,' I said jumping up. 'We've got to go. Mum will go crazy if we're late.'

Alice got up too.

'Sorry, Bruno.' she said, 'We're like the story of

Cinderella.'

I laughed.

'OK,' I said. 'I bags be Cinderella, and you can be the ugly sister.'

Alice made an ugly face and we all laughed. As I turned to go, my flip-flop fell off in the sand. Bruno picked it up.

'You lose your slipper, *Mademoiselle*,' he said.

I grinned as I took it.

'*Merci*,' I said, in my best French accent. Then Alice and I waved good-bye to Bruno, and raced along the beach.

'What do you think about Pascal now?' I asked Alice.

'He's very good-looking?'

'True. But we knew that already. I want to know what you really think of him, now that you know him a bit better.'

Alice sighed.

'He's a bit of a pain?'

'You're nearly right. He's a total pain.'

Alice looked like she was going to argue, and then she changed her mind.

'You're right,' she said. 'He's a total pain. But I *so* don't want to talk about it.'

I really wanted to talk about it, but I could see that Alice had her stubborn look on, and I knew I wouldn't get anywhere.

Alice started to run.

'I'll race you home,' she said. 'Last one there gets extra stew.'

I raced after her. It had been a very interesting morning.

Chapter Twenty-Three

The next day was the last day before we had to leave to catch the boat home. Alice and I woke up early, but didn't bother getting up. We lay in our cute little attic bedroom and chatted.

'At least we don't have to hang out with Bruno today,' said Alice after a while.

'But I told him we'd meet him,' I protested.

Alice shrugged.

'So? We can just not show up, can't we? It's not like we're ever going to see him again, is it?'

Suddenly the thought of never seeing Bruno again made me feel kind of sad, even though I wasn't sure why.

Alice was laughing.

'It's not like you *want* to meet him or anything is it? I mean we both know that he's a total loser.'

I didn't answer immediately. I didn't know exactly how it had happened, but I realised that I didn't think of Bruno as a loser-boy any more. He was really nice, and I was looking forward to meeting him again.

'But—' I began, but Alice interrupted.

'After all, now that we don't want to see Pascal, what's the point in hanging out with Bruno?'

Because he's fun?

Because I like him?

Because I told him we'd meet him again?

Because he'd promised not to wear the yellow shorts, and without them, Alice might be able to see the real Bruno?

Because—

Before I could think of the right thing to say to Alice, Dad shouted up the stairs.

'Megan, Alice,' he called. 'Get up. It's our last full day, and we don't want to waste one single second of it.'

Alice and I got dressed quickly and stumbled down the stairs. If it was our last day, why couldn't we just relax and enjoy it? Why did we have to do stuff?

Dad had already been to the bakery, and the kitchen was full of the smell of yummy warm bread.

'Fido says *bonjour*,' Dad said when he saw Alice and me.

I made a face.

'Dad, you are *so* not funny. You know well that his name is Bruno.'

Alice laughed like Dad was the funniest person on earth though, and Dad looked pleased. Alice can be such a goody-goody sometimes.

Mum smiled at us.

'Sounds like you two are getting very friendly

with this Bruno.'

Alice smiled back at her.

'Oh, it's not me,' she said quickly. 'It's Megan. Megan's very, very friendly with him.'

I should have said something funny back to Alice, but I couldn't think of anything. And besides, I could feel my face going red, and I didn't want anyone to ask me why. How could I tell them why my face was red, when I didn't even know myself?

And if Mum saw my red face, she'd know it was something to do with Bruno.

And if she knew that Bruno was making my face go red, she'd never be able to resist giving me a big, long, embarrassing talk about feelings. She would *never* let me hear the end of it.

Dad saved me by shoving a basket of bread into my hands.

'Take that outside,' he said, and I felt like hugging him for being the kind of person who doesn't notice stuff like daughters with faces the colour of over-ripe tomatoes.

We ate our breakfast on the terrace outside.

'Well,' said Mum, as she sipped the last of her green tea. 'What are we going to do for our last day in France?'

'Beach,' said Rosie. 'Please, please, please can we go to the beach? I want to build the biggest sand-castle ever.'

Dad had other ideas.

'There's one museum that we just have to see. It's not too far, and it's very, very educational. You girls will love it, I know.'

I made a face at Alice and she made one back at me. We *so* did not need to see another museum. I thought I'd die if I had to look at another grey map with lots of stupid pins stuck in it. This was supposed to be a holiday, wasn't it? Not a big long history lesson. I was fairly sure that Grace and her friend weren't visiting museums in Lanzarote. They were probably doing totally cool stuff all the time, and as soon as

Alice heard about it, she'd be sorry that she'd come on holidays with a loser family like mine.

I looked at Dad.

'Can we do something else? Please?' I said.

Dad shrugged.

'I suppose you two can do whatever you like,' he said. 'But I've made up my mind. I'm going to the museum. What about you Sheila?'

Everyone looked at Mum. Suddenly I remembered hearing her talking to her sister Linda on the phone, the day before we came to France.

'I'm really looking forward to the holiday,' she'd said. 'But I hope Donal doesn't insist on dragging us around loads of awful boring museums.'

I smiled at the thought, but then I remembered that Mum has this stupid idea that parents should back each other up, whenever the kids are listening, so she just said.

'The museum sounds good to me. You can never have enough history, can you?'

Rosie folded her arms in a pout.

'Beach,' she said in a sulky voice.

Mum smiled at her.

'If you're a good girl, and stop sulking,' she said. 'We can go to the beach after the museum. We have two cans of chick peas left, and I can make a nice salad, so we can have a picnic.'

Alice and I looked at each other again. Alice had been very understanding about Mum's food during the holidays, but there were limits. The poor girl had eaten more chick peas in the last nine days than she had in the previous thirteen years. Her face told me all I needed to know of her thoughts about a picnic that included chick peas.

'Er, Mum,' I said quickly. 'Why don't you and Dad and Rosie go to the museum? Alice and I can stay here.'

'Stay here and do what?' asked Dad.

'Em ...' I said.

'Em ...' Alice said.

'Well you're not staying here doing nothing,' said Mum. 'That would be a complete waste of time.'

'Oh, I just remembered,' said Alice. 'Megan and I want to meet Bruno one more time.'

I looked at her in surprise.

Hadn't she said she didn't want to meet Bruno?

What had happened to change her mind?

Still, I didn't really care. I was going to see Bruno again, and that was all that mattered.

I turned to Mum and Dad.

'Please, please, please, please, please?' I said.

Mum and Dad looked at each other, and finally Dad said,

'I suppose there's no harm in it. What do you think, Sheila?'

Mum shrugged.

'Well, the girls are thirteen now, so I suppose they'll be all right. Just promise to stay together. And wherever you go, be back here at six o'clock, at the very latest.'

'Yesss,' said Alice.

I didn't say anything. I was afraid that if Mum and Dad saw how happy we were, they might just change their minds and make us go with them to the museum.

* * *

Half an hour later, Mum and Dad and Rosie were packed up and ready to go. Alice and I went outside to wave good-bye to them.

'Are you *sure* you don't want me to leave you some of that nice chick pea salad?' said Mum. 'I've made plenty.'

'Sure we're sure,' I said. 'You have it. Alice and I will manage with whatever is left here.'

'OK,' said Mum. 'Now remember if you're going out, take some food with you. I don't want you buying any rubbish while I'm not here to keep an eye on you. There's bread and cheese, and there's also some of those nice red apples.'

'Yes, Mum,' I said.

By now Dad was revving up the car, but Mum wasn't finished yet.

'Oh, and there's a bit of last night's lentil stew in the fridge. That would be nice for you. It doesn't matter that it's cold.'

At the other side of the car I could see Alice pretending to vomit. She was right. Warm lentil stew was bad enough. Cold lentil stew was too gross to even think about.

Mum kept talking.

'And drink plenty of water. You need it in this hot weather. And—'

Then Dad saved us.

'Sheila, if we don't go now there will be no point going at all. I want to see every single thing in the museum.'

'OK. OK,' said Mum. 'I just don't want the girls to go hungry or thirsty.'

She turned back to me.

'Now be good girls. And we'll see you back here at six. And don't forget ......'

We never got to hear what we weren't supposed to forget, because Dad forgot that Mum
was talking and he drove off in the middle of her
sentence. Seconds later they were out of sight.

'Yesss,' said Alice. 'Free at last.'

'I still can't believe they left us here on our
own,' I said. 'I wonder why Mum suddenly feels
we're so grown up? She usually treats me like I'm
a total baby.'

Alice laughed.

'Stop wondering, and start enjoying it,' she
said. 'Now, last one in the back garden gets the
broken deck-chair.'

So we raced around to the back of the house
to enjoy our day of freedom.

Chapter Twenty-Four

Much later, after Alice and I had played loads of games of cards and Scrabble, I lay on my back and looked up into the trees.

'We'll have to go soon,' I said. 'Bruno will be waiting for us.'

Alice giggled.

'Bruno who?' she asked.

I threw a handful of grass over her face.

'How many Brunos do you know?' I asked.

'Besides my granny's dog?' asked Alice as she threw a bigger handful of grass over my face.

I sat up and brushed the grass off me.

'Anyway, whatever his name is, we have to go and meet him.'

Alice patted me on the shoulder like I was a baby.

'Megan, you are *so* gullible,' she said. 'We're not meeting Bruno.'

'But you said—'

She interrupted me.

'I'm not totally stupid. I know what I said. But that was just so your mum and dad would get off our backs and go away and leave us alone.'

She stopped talking and looked at me real closely. I felt uncomfortable, and turned away, but I knew she was still staring at me.

'Hey,' she said. 'What's with you and Bruno? You don't actually *like* him do you?'

I put my head down and pretended to be interested in pulling a few stray pieces of grass from my hair. Alice wasn't fooled for a second.

'He's such a *total* loser, Megan. Please tell me you don't like him.'

I still didn't answer. After all, what could I say? Alice thought Bruno was a loser, and nothing I could say would ever change that. And if she thought I liked a loser, she'd never, ever stop going on about it. Alice isn't very good at forgetting stuff like that.

Then I remembered Pascal. Alice had really, really liked him, and when he turned out to be the biggest pain in the history of the world, she wasn't one bit embarrassed.

And when we were at summer camp, she sneaked out and got into loads of trouble because she wanted to meet Lee, and he turned out to be a bit of a pain, and she wasn't embarrassed about that either.

So why was I embarrassed about liking Bruno who was perfectly nice?

Suddenly I felt brave.

'Bruno's OK, actually,' I said, trying to make it sound like I didn't really care one way or the other.

Alice gave a big laugh.

'OK for a total loser, you mean.'

I didn't answer, so Alice continued.

'Look at the facts, Megan. What's there to like about Bruno? He's got a dog's name. He wears loser clothes. He looks like a loser. He talks like a loser. So guess what? He's a loser.'

She was all wrong. (Except for the bit about the dog's name, and that really wasn't his fault.)

At first I was going to argue with her, but then I changed my mind. I'd suddenly had a bad thought. If a miracle happened, and I actually managed to convince Alice that Bruno was nice, then we'd have to go and meet him.

And if we went to meet him, what would I say to him?

Alice would be watching me, and saving up stuff to tease me with.

It would all be too embarrassing even to think about.

And all of a sudden I wasn't brave anymore.

'Yeah, you're right,' I said. 'I was just kidding. Bruno really is a loser.'

Alice giggled.

'Yeah. A loser in yellow shorts.'

I felt kind of bad, like I'd betrayed Bruno or something.

But not bad enough to do anything about it.

I lay down again. It was nice just lying there, watching the leaves rustling in the warm breeze.

'I feel lazy,' I said after a while. 'And a whole afternoon lying here sounds just perfect.'

'A whole afternoon lying here?' Alice said it like I'd suggested that we jump off a cliff or something.

'But, you said—'

Alice interrupted me.

'Keep up, Megan. I said we're not meeting Bruno, but that doesn't mean we have to stay here. Here is boring. And it's our last day. Let's go off and have an adventure.'

I didn't much like the sound of that. Alice's

adventures usually ended up as disasters.

'An adventure?' I repeated.

'Yes. An adventure,' said Alice firmly. 'An adventure is just what we need to finish off this holiday.'

'Like what kind of adventure?'

Alice sighed. 'You can be such a scaredy cat sometimes, Megan.'

I *hate* it when Alice calls me a scaredy cat. (It doesn't make any difference that she's usually right.)

I folded my arms and didn't say anything.

'Sorry, Meg,' said Alice, when she saw my face. 'I promised not to call you that any more didn't I?'

I nodded.

'Only about a thousand times,' I said.

Alice smiled.

'Sorry. I won't do it anymore. I promise. Anyway, we're not really going on an adventure. I was only winding you up. Why don't we just take our bikes out and go for a cycle? It'll be fun to see a bit more of this place before we leave. And we needn't go far.'

I smiled too. A cycle around the countryside didn't sound too scary. Even my mum wouldn't have a problem with that.

'That's settled, so,' said Alice jumping up. 'Now let's get ready.'

I followed her into the house.

'Do you fancy bringing some lentil stew?' I asked, grinning.

Alice pretended she had to think about it.

'Em ...... no. Not today thanks. Actually, not ever, thanks. I don't suppose your Mum has hidden a double cheese pizza in the freezer?'

I shook my head.

'No chance. Will we bring those apples? Or maybe some bread and cheese?'

'No,' said Alice. 'I'm not even hungry. Are you?'

I shrugged.

'Not really.'

'Well then, no point in bringing food, is there? Anyway, I have money, so if we get hungry later we can buy something to eat,' said Alice.

'Sounds good to me,' I said. 'Now let's get going, before Mum and Dad get back.'

As we wheeled our bikes down the driveway of the house, I suddenly stopped.

'Hang on a sec,' I said. 'I've forgotten my jumper.'

Alice laughed.

'It's roasting,' she said. 'What do you want a jumper for?'

I shrugged.

'It might get cold later,' I said, trying hard not to sound like my mother.

Alice kept walking.

'Later is ages away,' she said. 'And later we'll be back here, so you don't need to bring your jumper with you, do you?'

Mum always insists that I bring a jumper with

me whenever I go out, even on baking hot days, and it's a hard habit to break. But it wasn't worth arguing about.

So we got on our bikes, and cycled off.

Chapter Twenty-Five

We cycled towards the village. I didn't want to go past the bakery, in case we'd bump into Bruno, but there didn't seem to be any other way to go. Luckily only Serge, Bruno's little brother, was standing outside in the dusty street. Alice waved at him, and

he stuck his tongue out at us in reply.

Alice braked hard.

'He's a cheeky thing,' she said. 'Do you think we should stop and threaten him?'

I *so* didn't want to stop right there outside the bakery. If Bruno saw us, he'd wonder why we weren't calling for him.

How could I explain that even thinking about him made me feel embarrassed?

How could I explain that Alice thought he was a loser, and that I was too much of a coward to try to change her mind?

It was much easier to keep on cycling, and to pretend that Bruno didn't even exist.

'Serge is just a spoiled brat,' I said. 'Forget about him, and let's keep going. We're meant to be on an adventure, aren't we?'

Alice laughed and began to pedal faster. I followed her as quickly as I could.

When we got to the end of the village, we stopped at a crossroads. We'd never been this far on our own before.

'Where now?' I asked.

Alice shrugged.

'Dunno. Which way did your parents go?'

I looked at the signposts, and then pointed to the left.

'That way, I think.'

Alice grinned.

'OK, that settles it. We're not taking that road. We don't want to accidentally end up at your dad's totally cool museum, do we?'

I smiled.

'But we could all sit down together and talk about the environment, and then we could share that lovely chick pea salad.'

Alice made a face.

'Thanks, but no thanks,' she said. 'Now which of these other roads will we choose?'

Now I shrugged.

'They all look much the same to me. I've never heard of any of these places. How about that one?' I said, pointing to the smallest, quietest road.

'Sounds fine to me,' said Alice, climbing on to her bike.

'Wait,' I said. 'How will we find our way back? We haven't got a map or anything.'

Alice giggled.

'Your dad has lots of maps, and how many times has he got lost this holiday?'

I giggled too.

'Lots of times?'

'Exactly,' said Alice. 'So when we're coming back, we'll just follow the signposts for our village, and we'll be OK.'

'You're sure?'

'Sure, I'm sure! Now let's go. We've only got a few hours of freedom left.'

*   *   *

We cycled along for ages. It was kind of fun, not knowing exactly where we were going, or what we were going to do when we got there. I felt happy and free and I was really glad that Alice had persuaded me to come. If it had been up to me, we'd have stayed in the garden for the whole day, and how boring would that have been?

As we cycled, we chatted about all kinds of stuff – about the boat-trip home, about secondary school, and about Melissa of course. Alice told me a really funny story about a girl who'd been in her class in Dublin, and I had to stop cycling for a while, I was laughing so much.

Soon we came to a tiny little village. There was a little old lady sitting outside the only shop, knitting something huge out of disgusting mustard-coloured wool.

'There's your mother's long-lost sister,' said Alice, making me laugh again.

'Will we stop and get something to eat?' I suggested, as soon as I was able to talk. 'Maybe that lady would make us a sandwich or something.'

Alice shook her head.

'Nah. I'm not even hungry yet. And that lady

doesn't look like she's going anywhere any time soon. Let's go on for another bit, and we can come back here later and buy stuff. OK?'

I nodded. I was having so much fun that nothing, not even food, seemed to matter too much.

After another few kilometres or so, we came to a forest. Alice braked and skidded to a halt. I braked a second too late, and skidded into her. I picked up my bike, and rubbed my arm where it had bumped off Alice's handlebars.

'Watch it,' I said. 'How about you warn me when you're going to stop?'

'Sorry, Meg,' said Alice. 'I didn't have time to warn you. It's just that this forest is so cool. It's just like the enchanted forest in a story book I had when I was small. It was my favourite book for ages.'

I forgot about the pain in my arm. Alice was right. The forest did look kind of enchanted. It was quiet and dark and mysterious.

'Let's go inside and explore,' said Alice.

'Maybe we'll find Sleeping Beauty, or Snow White or someone.'

I gave her a small push.

'You are *so* boring,' I said. 'Who needs Snow White? I hope we find Prince Charming, or maybe even Bruno's handsome cousin Pascal.'

Alice laughed.

'Yuck,' she said. 'He's no Prince Charming, that's for sure. Prince Totally-Not-Charming, he is. Now come on. Let's go and start our adventure. Did you bring the bicycle locks?'

I shook my head.

'I thought you had them.'

'I thought *you* had them,' repeated Alice. 'Anyway, it doesn't matter. We can just leave the bikes here. There's no one around.'

'But we can't do that,' I protested. 'If someone did come along and take our bikes, how would we get back? It's much too far to walk. And besides, Mum and Dad will kill me if my bike gets stolen.'

'That wouldn't be your fault. It would be the thief's fault for being so dishonest,' said Alice.

I sighed.

'You know that's not how Mum and Dad would see it. They'd say it was my fault for being careless.'

'OK, OK,' said Alice. 'We're wasting precious time here. Why don't we just wheel the bikes a bit of the way in to the forest? We can hide them under some branches, and then even if someone comes along, they won't see them. And if they don't see them, they can't steal them, can they?'

I sighed again. She was right as usual.

I followed Alice as she wheeled her bike in amongst the trees. It was cool there, out of the sunshine. The ground was soft and springy under our feet. There was a smell of Christmas.

Soon Alice stopped near a big tree.

'This is perfect,' she said.

We propped our bikes against the tree, and

dragged some old branches over them to cam-
ouflage them.

When we were finished, I stood back and
looked at our work.

'Excellent,' I said. 'You'd never guess there
were bikes hidden there. It looks just like a pile
of old branches.'

Alice grinned.

'Now that's sorted, let's go explore.'

Chapter Twenty-Six

We wandered through the forest for ages. Alice made up a big, long story about two kidnapped pop stars, who escaped from their kidnappers, and had to survive for weeks on their own. When rescuers found them, they were almost dead, but they were keeping their spirits

up by taking turns to sing songs from their hit album.

Alice is great at that kind of stuff, and after a while, I almost believed that I *was* one of the pop stars, and I found myself ducking behind trees, at every sudden gust of wind, or every crackle of twigs beneath our feet.

Soon though, I stopped feeling that I was a pop star, and I felt more like a tired and hungry schoolgirl.

I stopped walking, and threw myself down on a pile of soft, mossy stuff.

'Wait, Al,' I said. 'I need to rest for a while.'

Alice came back and sat beside me.

'I'm a bit tired too,' she said. 'Let's rest for a while, and then we can go back and go to that small shop and buy some food.'

So we rested for a while.

'A toasted cheese sandwich,' said Alice. 'I can smell it already.'

I closed my eyes.

'Pizza,' I said. 'With extra cheese – loads and loads of extra cheese, and pepperoni.'

'Yuck,' said Alice. 'I'd like chips – with heaps of salt and vinegar.'

My mouth was beginning to water.

'Stop, Al,' I said. 'Please stop. How about we stop talking about food, and actually go and get some?'

Alice grinned.

'Sounds good to me.'

So we stood up, dusted ourselves off, and began to walk, with Alice leading the way – striding quickly like she always does.

We had walked for quite a bit, when I noticed that Alice wasn't moving as confidently as she had at first.

'What's wrong?' I asked.

Alice turned back to look at me.

'Nothing,' she said. 'Why?'

'Oh, no reason,' I said, and we walked some more.

Soon Alice stopped and began to look around. I was starting to get worried now.

'Al, what's wrong?' I said again.

'I'm just ...' said Alice, as she started to walk. Then she stopped, and turned around and walked the other way.

'You're just what?'

'I'm just not sure which is the way out of here.' Her voice was unusually quiet.

I gulped.

'But ... But ... I don't know the way either. What are we going to do?'

Alice put her hand on my arm.

'Well, we won't worry, that's for sure,' she said. 'After all, how big can this forest be?'

I gulped again.

'Don't you remember, Al? The other day Dad was reading from his guide book, and he said there was a forest in this area that covers eleven thousand hectares. Do you think this could be it?'

'I don't know, do I?'

'Do you know how big a hectare is?' I asked.

Alice shook her head.

'Sorry. No idea. If we did that stuff at school, I wasn't listening. But maybe it's really small, like a centimetre or something.'

'Yeah, or maybe it's really big, like a kilometre or something. Oh, Al. What are we going to do?'

Alice hugged me.

'We're just being silly. We haven't really tried to find our way out yet.'

Suddenly I had an idea.

'What about your watch – the super-duper fancy one your Mum gave you for your birthday? Hasn't that got a compass on it?'

Alice looked at her watch, and made a face.

'No. I could tell you the time in San Francisco, or Moscow, but I can't use my watch to help us get out of here. We'll have to think of something else. You should know though – you read lots of books. What do kids do when they get lost in forests?'

I had to smile. In the kind of books I liked, kids only got lost in department stores, and airports and places like that, and they were always rescued by kind security guards. I wasn't admitting that to Alice though.

'Weeeell,' I said. 'Usually they start by following the sun.'

We both looked up. The small patches of sky that we could see through the trees were grey. What had happened to the lovely sunny day?

'OK, so following the sun isn't going to work for us today,' I said. 'But that's not the only solution. I read a book once, where kids followed a stream, and found their way home.'

I'd just made that up, but I thought it sounded good. It made sense really. All streams end up in the sea don't they? And the sea was near our house. That had to be the answer.

Alice sighed.

'No chance of finding a stream. There's a drought, remember? It hasn't rained here for weeks, so all the streams will have dried up.'

'Well, then, we just have to walk in a straight line, until we come to the edge of the forest. Easy,' I said, a bit more confidently than I felt.

Alice smiled at me.

'See, Megan. I love that you're always the sensible one. I knew I could count on you in a crisis. Now lead us out of here.'

Chapter Twenty-Seven

S o, there I was, lost in the middle of a huge forest, and instead of leading the way, as she usually did, Alice was relying on me to show her the way home.

Brilliant.

Totally, totally brilliant.

I looked all around me carefully, trying to find something different, something I'd recognise again, if we walked past it a second time. I was wasting my time though. We were in the middle of a forest, and there was nothing to see except trees.

I took a deep breath, and started to walk. I took my time, concentrating on going in a straight line. Alice walked right behind me, encouraging me, like she did when I was learning to roller-blade.

'Keep it up, Megan. You're doing great,' she kept saying.

And even though I knew I wasn't doing great, it made me feel a bit better.

Every now and then, a tree would block my path, and I had to carefully walk around it, and then try to keep walking in the same direction as before. Soon Alice began to walk beside me, and I wasn't so scared any more. For a while it felt like we were just out for any old walk, and that we weren't lost at all.

We started to chat again.

'What do you think Melissa would do in this situation?' asked Alice.

I thought for a minute.

'Worry that her hair would get messed up by all these branches?' I said, as I flicked yet another branch out of my face.

Alice laughed.

'Yeah, or cry because she got a speck of dirt on her sandals.'

We spent a while listing all the stupid things that Melissa would do if she was in our situation, but in the end, we both ran out of ideas. Then I started to get scared again. My legs were getting tired too.

'Let's stop for a while,' I said.

Alice shook her head.

'Maybe we should keep going,' she said.

And that's when I realised that she was scared too.

And that's when I started to get very, very scared.

Alice is the bravest girl I've ever known.

And if Alice was scared, then, things were very, very, very bad.

I pulled Alice's arm, and made her stop.

'Wait,' I said. 'Are we even sure that we're going in a straight line?'

'Of course we are,' said Alice. 'I think.'

I looked up through the trees, but there was still no sign of the sun. I tried not to sound too scared.

'Let's be double careful,' I said. 'Let's both watch out and make sure that we are walking in a straight line. OK?'

Alice nodded.

'OK.'

And so we walked some more.

Much, much later, when I felt like my legs were going to fall off, I stopped and leaned against a tree.

'Look,' I said. 'Doesn't this tree look familiar to you?'

Alice sighed.

'I don't know,' she said. 'It's a tree. It's green and brown, just like all the others.'

'Look properly,' I said. 'Look at this broken branch. Haven't we seen this before?'

Alice shook her head.

'I don't know. Maybe. There's lots of trees

with broken branches.'

I looked around. Alice was right. There were lots of trees just like this one. I thought hard.

'We should leave a trail,' I said.

'Like Hansel and Gretel? They used crumbs, didn't they? We don't have any bread. And if we did, I wouldn't scatter it on the ground, I'd eat it.'

'Yeah, but Hansel and Gretel used pebbles first, remember?'

'But there are no pebbles here either.'

Once again she was right. There wasn't a single stone to be seen. Except for Alice and me, there was nothing to be seen except for trees and mossy stuff.

We had to do something though. We had to know if we were walking in a straight line. Suddenly I had an idea. I reached up and broke two twigs off a tree.

'Look,' I said. 'How about if we put these on the ground in a cross shape, and that will leave a trail?'

'That's a great idea,' said Alice, and for one second I felt proud, before I started to feel scared again.

Alice reached up and pulled off loads of twigs.

'OK,' she said. 'You go first, and we can do every second one.'

And so we continued to walk, marking our path every few metres with two crossed twigs. After a while, my hands were cut from breaking twigs, my back was sore from bending down making the crosses, and my legs felt like I'd been walking for about a hundred years.

I stopped to catch my breath.

'What time is it?' I asked.

Alice looked at her stupid fancy watch that didn't have a compass.

'It's ten past five,' she said.

That was very bad news. Even if we found our bikes immediately, we wouldn't be back home by six. Mum was going to kill us.

'Alice—' I began, but she interrupted me.

'Let's keep walking for ten more minutes, and then we'll stop for a rest. OK?'

I nodded. All I wanted to do was get out of there, and get home as fast as I could.

Just then Alice stopped so suddenly that I crashed into her.

'That wasn't ten minutes, was it?' I said.

Alice didn't reply.

'Why have we stopped?' I asked.

Instead of replying, she pointed down at the ground.

I followed her pointed finger, and gulped. There on the ground in front of Alice, were two neatly crossed twigs.

'Maybe someone else did that,' I suggested. 'Or maybe they just fell off the tree like that.' Alice walked a few metres and pointed again – two more neatly crossed twigs. I ran past her and saw two more.

I threw myself down on the mossy ground.

'We're going around in a circle,' I said, trying not to cry.

'Remind me again why Hansel and Gretel left a trail,' said Alice.

'So they could follow it home,' I said.

'So starting it when ...' she began.

I finished her sentence for her.

'... we were already lost was a total waste of time. If we follow these twigs, we'll just end up walking in an endless circle. It was a stupid, stupid idea. I am *so* dumb sometimes.'

Alice sat down and put her arm around me.

'You're not dumb,' she said. 'You're the cleverest girl I know.'

'So why did I suggest a stupid trail then?' I asked.

'Well, at least now we know we're walking around in circles,' she said.

'And knowing that will help us how exactly?'

'Weeeell,' said Alice slowly. 'Now we know that we have to do something different.'

'Like what?'

Alice put her head down.

'Sorry, Meg,' she said. 'I don't know. I don't know what to do.'

Neither of us said anything for a while. Suddenly I jumped up. 'We are *so* totally stupid,' I said. 'Why didn't we think of it before?'

'Think of what?'

'Why don't we just use your phone and phone someone for help?'

Alice still kept her head down.

'I'm out of credit, remember? I used the last of it to text Grace in Lanzarote the other day.'

'I know,' I said. 'But even without credit you can phone the police. Even I know that.'

Alice still didn't look up.

'I know that too, but because I'm out of credit, I left my phone back at the house. I didn't see any point in bringing it.'

I sat down again. I didn't want to think of Grace having fun in Lanzarote, but I couldn't help it.

'I bet you wish you were in Lanzarote now,' I said.

Alice looked up at last and gave me a small smile.

'Not really,' she said. 'Who needs Lanzarote? I'd be happy to be back at your place, running around the garden, playing with Rosie.'

Suddenly that sounded like the best thing in the whole world – just being out of this forest, and safe again.

And it also felt like the most impossible thing in the whole world.

Chapter Twenty-Eight

We stayed sitting down for a very long time. There didn't seem to be much point in walking, since we hadn't the faintest idea which way we should walk.

'Are you hungry?' I said after a while.

'A bit,' said Alice.

'A bit? You're only a bit hungry?'

'OK. OK. So I'm very hungry,' she said.

'Me too. I wish we'd brought that food Mum left for us.'

'That was my fault,' said Alice glumly. 'You wanted to but I told you not to. You didn't sneak

an apple into your pocket, when I wasn't looking, did you?'

I shook my head.

Alice put her hand into her pocket, and pulled
out her money.

'I've got forty-two euro. I think I'd pay all of
that for one slice of pizza right now.'

'I'm so hungry, I'd pay all of that for an apple
right now,' I said.

'Or one slice of bread.'

I had to giggle.

'A plate of Mum's lentil stew.'

Alice giggled too.

'Chick pea salad.'

'Stop,' I said. 'I don't think I've ever been so
hungry in my entire life. Do you think we could
starve to death?'

'Nah. We could easily survive for a few days.
We—'

She stopped talking when she saw my face.

'But we won't have to survive for a few days.

We'll be out of here soon. Don't worry.'

I wanted to believe her, but couldn't. I looked around.

'There's probably lots of stuff here that we could eat,' I said.

Alice picked up a handful of moss and dead leaves.

'Even if we found something that looked nice,' she said. 'How would we know if it was safe to eat? We'd probably both have to eat different things, just in case one of the things was poisonous. Then at least one of us would survive.'

I shook my head.

'No way. I'm scared enough already. What would I do if you died of poisoning and I was stuck out here all on my own? Or if you got really sick – I'd never be able to carry you.'

Alice jumped up.

'This is totally stupid,' she said. 'Why are we talking about starving to death, or being poisoned? We're just being drama queens. And sitting here isn't getting us anywhere. Let's go.'

'But what if we're walking in the wrong direction?' I asked.

Alice stamped her foot.

'At least we'll be walking. We can't just sit here.'

And with that, she marched off. I hesitated for a second, and then I jumped up and followed her. Alice might be grumpy, but I *so* wasn't staying there on my own.

We walked for ages – so long that I could feel giant blisters growing on my toes. Why hadn't I listened when Mum told me to wear socks that morning? Alice was leading the way now, and I followed her. We didn't talk – there didn't seem to be much that we could say. After a while, Alice seemed to be almost running, and I was struggling to keep up.

In the end, I couldn't take any more.

'Al,' I said. 'Please stop.'

Alice turned back to me, while still walking

quickly ahead.

'We can't…….' she began.

'Look out,' I called – but it was too late. Alice stumbled over a large log, and crashed to the ground. I raced over to her.

'Al, are you OK? Please be OK.'

She opened her eyes and groaned.

'Yes, I think I'm OK. But my ankle hurts.'

I held my hand out to her.

'Here,' I said. 'Let me help you up.'

Alice took my hand and staggered up on to one foot.

'Can you put your other foot down?' I asked.

Alice nodded grimly.

'Sure I can.' But when she did as I suggested, her face crumpled up in pain.

'Sorry,' she said. 'It doesn't look like I can put it down after all.'

She leaned against a tree for balance, and sat down on the log that she had tripped over. Her face was gone a horrible grey-white colour, like leftover porridge.

I sat down beside her and burst into tears. Alice put her arm around me.

'Hey,' she said. 'I'm the one who's hurt here. I'm the one who should be crying.'

'I know,' I sobbed. 'And I'm sorry, Alice. But I'm afraid. I'm really, really afraid.'

Alice hugged me tight.

'Look, everything's going to be OK,' she said. She looked at her watch. 'It's almost six o'clock, and we should be home by now. And you know what your Mum is like. By half six, she'll have called the police.'

I shook my head.

'Obviously you don't know what my mum is like. She'll have called the police by five past six.'

'Well then,' said Alice. 'Then there's nothing to worry about, is there? The police will find us.'

'Why did we have to hide our bikes so well? If they were just on the roadway, at least the police would know we were in here. How on earth are they going to find us now?'

'I don't know. But they'll have machines for finding people, or something. Anyway, let's let them worry about that. It is their job. All we have to do is sit here and wait.'

So that's what we did.

Chapter Twenty-Nine

It was nearly seven o'clock. It was starting to get darker, and the forest was getting creepy. A few times, Alice had tried to walk, but even when she leaned on me, it was totally impossible.

'What's that?' I said, jumping as I heard a rustle behind me.

Alice looked around.

'There's nothing there. It's just the wind in the trees.'

I clung on to Alice.

'I keep hearing weird noises,' I said.

Alice smiled.

'That'll just be my stomach rumbling.'

I tried to smile too, but I couldn't.

'What if the police can't find us?' I asked. 'Did you ever hear of anyone getting lost in a forest and never being found?'

Alice shook her head.

'Nah. That only happens in fairy tales. And in fairy tales it only happens to bad people, and we're not bad people, so we don't have to worry.'

'We *are* bad though. We're always saying mean things about Melissa.'

Alice shrugged.

'She deserves it, so she doesn't count. You know, Meg, I'd really love to see Melissa now. I'd love to see her come prancing along in her high heels.'

I nodded.

'Yeah, me too. I think if we get out of here, I'll never be mean to Melissa again.'

Alice giggled.

'Let's not make any foolish promises,' she said. 'Remember, tomorrow we'll look back on this as a big adventure.'

'Well, I wish tomorrow would hurry up and come, because I'm not having much fun now,' I said.

*　　　*　　　*

It was half past nine, and Alice and I were huddled together trying to keep warm.

'I've been thinking about Bruno,' said Alice suddenly.

I'd just been thinking about him too, but there was *no* way I was telling Alice that.

'What were you thinking?' I asked casually.

'I was thinking that Pascal was really mean to him today when he pushed him down on the sand. I should have done something.'

I nodded.

'I was surprised that you did nothing.'
Alice sighed.

'I was still trying to convince myself that

Pascal was nice.'

I shook my head.

'He is *so* not nice. Oh, and I forgot to tell you about Pascal and the yellow shorts.'

Now Alice sat up straight.

'You mean those gross yellow shorts that seemed to be glued to Bruno?'

I giggled.

'Yes. They're the ones. Bruno told me that Pascal got them somewhere. He gave them to Bruno, and convinced him that they were totally cool, and persuaded him to wear them every day.'

Alice gasped.

'He's a big, fat, ugly pig,' she said, 'He wears cool stuff himself, so he knows what's nice. He *knew* those shorts were totally gross. What a mean, mean thing to do.'

I shrugged.

'Not much we can do about it now.'

Alice spoke fiercely.

'Yes, there is. I promise you, if I get out of here, I'll pay that evil boy back.'

I shrugged again.

'Let's get out of here first, then we can worry about that.'

Just then a cold wind blew. I shivered

'I so wish I'd brought my fleece,' I said for the hundredth time.

'Me too,' said Alice for the hundredth time.

'Is your ankle very sore?'

'No,' said Alice bravely. 'It's fine.'

I knew she was lying. If her ankle was better, she'd be racing through the forest now, she wouldn't be sitting down waiting for someone to find us.

Suddenly there was a horrible howling noise. I screeched.

'What is it? What is it?'

Alice tried to look around, but that was a bit of a waste of time since it was completely dark by now.

'It's just a bird or something,' she said.

'I've never heard a bird make a noise like that,' I said. 'Do you think it might be a wolf?'

'Nah,' said Alice. 'I don't think there are any wolves in France.'

'There are,' I said. 'Don't you remember Dad telling Rosie about them the other day?'

'He was just trying to get her to come in from the garden and go to bed,' said Alice.

'Maybe,' I said. 'But that doesn't mean there aren't wolves around here. There could be whole packs of them out there, waiting for us to fall asleep, so they can attack.'

Alice hugged me.

'Now you're just being silly,' she said. 'Why don't we talk about Melissa for a while, to make ourselves feel better?'

I shook my head.

'I'm not going to say anything bad about her any more, remember?'

'Oh yeah,' said Alice. 'I forgot. What can we

talk about so? Food?'

'No way. My stomach hurts I'm so hungry.'

'Family?' asked Alice.

'Double no way. Mum and Dad are going to kill me when we get back.'

'Do you think they'll ever let you out on your own again?'

I shrugged.

'I don't know, and I don't care. After this I don't ever want to go out on my own again. I'm going to stay home where I'll be safe.'

A little bit after this, Alice started to cry.

'It's all my fault,' she said. 'We should have gone to the stupid museum with your mum and dad.'

I felt like crying too, but now it looked like I'd have to pretend to be strong.

'Hey,' I said. 'I didn't want to go to the museum either, remember?'

'Maybe. But if it was up to you, we'd have stayed at the house. Coming out here was all my stupid, stupid idea. Oh, Meg, what are we going to do? We're stuck out here, we're freezing and starving, and my leg hurts, and I just want to go home.'

Now Alice started to sob so much that I could feel her shaking next to me. I put both my arms around her.

'It's OK, Al,' I said. 'Don't worry. We'll be out of here soon.'

'Do you really think so?' said Alice through her sobs.

'Of course I think so,' I said, with my fingers crossed so the lie wouldn't seem so bad. 'We'll be home before you know it.'

Chapter Thirty

Alice's super-duper watch had a light on it, so I knew it was nearly eleven o'clock. I'd never before been out so late without an adult, and I so wasn't enjoying it.

I had piled a big heap of moss on the ground, and Alice and I were huddled together on it, trying to keep warm. We weren't talking very much. For the first time in our whole lives, we had run out of things to say.

Suddenly Alice sat up.

'What was that noise?' she hissed.

I was so cold and hungry I'd forgotten about being scared for a while, but now I was terrified all over again. I clung on to Alice.

'Is it a wolf?' I said.

'Shhh. There it is again.'

I still couldn't hear anything.

'Did it sound like a wolf?' I asked.

'How am I supposed to know what a wolf sounds—' she began to say, then she grabbed me again. 'Can't you hear it now?' she whispered.

I shook my head.

'Maybe you're imagining it. It's probably just my stomach rumbling again. Or it could be my teeth chattering.'

'Shhh. There it is again,' said Alice. 'It's voices. Listen.'

At last I could hear it too – the sound of voices, far away and very faint. I jumped up.

'What's the French for "help"?' I asked.

Alice hobbled up to her feet, leaning on me for balance.

'Who cares?' she said.

Then she let out a screech that almost deafened me.

'Help! Help! We're over here! Help! Please help us!'

I shouted too.

'Help! Help! Over here! Help!'

There was silence, and then we could hear the voices once more, a bit closer this time.

Alice and I shouted and shouted. My throat began to hurt, but I didn't care. I forgot all about being cold and hungry and thirsty. Nothing mattered now except for getting out of the forest.

Soon we could see lights, and hear the sound of people trampling through the forest. Suddenly I had a really horrible thought.

'What if it's not the police?' I said. 'What if it's robbers or kidnappers?'

'At this moment, I don't really care,' said Alice. 'All I want to do is get out of here. So keep on shouting.'

She was right, so we shouted some more, until two very kind French policemen were standing beside us saying, 'Meg-anne? Al-eese?' and Alice and I were jumping up and down and trying not to hug them, we were so glad to see them.

One of the policemen carried Alice all the way to the road, which was only about a hundred metres from where we had been sitting. We should have felt really stupid, but we were much too happy for that.

When we got to their police car, the policemen gave us blankets to wrap ourselves up in. The blankets were a bit smelly, but I didn't care. I just wanted to be warm again.

Then one of the men pulled a big red apple from his pocket, and handed it to us with a smile.

'Hungry?' he said.

We didn't answer. Alice just grabbed the apple,

took a bite and then passed it to me. I took a bite and passed it back to her. And so we continued, until there were only pips and a stalk left. It wasn't the freshest, crispest apple I'd ever had, but that didn't matter right then. It tasted better than the yummiest cake I had ever eaten in my whole life.

Chapter Thirty-One

We got back to the house quickly – a bit too quickly. Now that I wasn't afraid of starvation or wolves anymore, it was time to be very, very afraid of Mum and Dad.

'I'll tell them it was all my fault,' said Alice.

'Thanks,' I said. 'But I don't think that will make much difference. I think they're going to kill me first and ask questions later.'

As we pulled up outside the house, the front door opened and Mum and Dad and Rosie came racing out. One of the policemen got out of the car and started to say something, but Mum just pushed him out of the way, opened the back door of the car and threw herself on top of me.

'My baby. My baby,' she said over and over again, hugging me and stroking my face and kissing me. Then, when she was finished that, she turned to Alice and did the same to her. Poor Alice didn't say anything, but I think she probably wished she was back in the forest again.

I got out of the car, and Dad came over to me. He had tears in his eyes, and that really scared me, because I have never, ever seen my dad cry. Then he hugged me for a very long time, while Rosie pulled at my arms and said,

'I'm glad you're back, Megan.'

The policemen patted Alice and me on the head, and then they drove away. Dad helped Alice into the house, and the rest of us trailed behind. Dad looked at Alice's ankle, and decided that it was just a sprain. Mum found a bandage in Lucy's first aid kit, and strapped it up.

'Now girls,' she said. 'You must be starving. Come to the table and get something to eat. Isn't it lucky that we didn't finish the lovely chick pea salad?'

Alice caught my eye and we grinned at each other. Neither of us said anything though, because seconds later we were shoving chick pea salad down our throats like we hadn't seen food for about a hundred years.

'How did the police find us?' asked Alice when she had finally stopped licking her plate.

'Well,' said Dad. 'When you didn't come home, we went and spoke to Bruno's family. Bruno's little brother had seen you in the village. He told Bruno, and he came into the street, and he saw which way you cycled.'

'So Bruno saved us?' said Alice.

Dad smiled.

'I suppose you could say that. In any case, later on, when we called the police, they had something to go on. They drove along the road you had taken, and they spoke to a shopkeeper who had seen you cycle past her shop.'

'Oh yes,' said Alice. 'I remember her. 'We were going to go back there later. Except ... well except we couldn't find the way.'

'Anyway,' continued Dad. 'That road is a dead end, and since the shopkeeper hadn't seen you cycle back, the police decided you must be in the forest somewhere. And that's how they found you.'

I couldn't join in the conversation. I still couldn't figure something out.

Why weren't Mum and Dad cross with us?

When we're at home, Mum goes crazy if I go next-door to Alice's place without telling her, so why was she so calm after I'd disappeared in a forest for half a day?

I decided I had to get it over with.

'Mum, Dad,' I said. 'Why aren't you cross with us?'

Mum got up and hugged and kissed me so much that I wondered if that was my punishment.

'We might be cross tomorrow, or the next day,' she said. 'But for now, we're just glad to have you home, safe and well.'

I still couldn't believe it was that simple.

'We went off without telling you where we were going. And we lied to you about spending the afternoon with Bruno. So tomorrow, am I going to be grounded forever?' I asked.

Mum and Dad looked at each other.

'How did you feel when you were in that forest?' asked Mum.

'I have never been so scared in my whole life,' I said. 'Or so cold or so hungry or so thirsty.'

Dad smiled.

'Maybe that's punishment enough then,' he said.

Then he came over and hugged me, and seconds later, Mum and Rosie and Alice joined in, and we hugged until I felt safe and warm and happy again.

Chapter Thirty-Two

Next morning Dad drove Alice and me to pick up our bikes. It was strange. Now that the sun was shining, and Dad was there with us, and we knew where we were going, the forest didn't seem like a scary place anymore.

Our bikes were there, exactly as we had left them. Alice was still resting her foot, so Dad and I tied the bikes on to the bike-rack, and then we went back home.

Mum was going crazy.

'Lucy left this place spotless for us,' she said. 'And it has to be spotless again. Take this mop, Megan, and wash the dining room floor, there's a good girl.'

An hour later, the house was sparkling clean. Lucky Alice couldn't do much, because of her ankle, so she had just sat on her bed, and folded and packed all of our clothes. When everything was ready, Mum made us all sit in the garden, so we wouldn't get the house messy again.

She looked at her watch.

'We've got an hour before we have to leave. Anyone want to do anything?'

Dad jumped up.

'There's this museum—' he began.

'No!' shouted everyone together.

Dad didn't seem too upset.

'I'll just sit here and read my book then.'

Alice stood up.

'Can Megan and I cycle in to the village one more time?'

Mum looked surprised.

'But your ankle?'

Alice smiled.

'It's almost better. And cycling won't hurt it a bit. And ... Er ... Sheila ... do you think we could take that bowl of lentil stew that's left in the fridge? Megan and I could have a quick picnic in the village.'

Mum beamed at her.

'That's a lovely idea, Alice. I'll pack it into a plastic bowl for you.'

Mum got up and went into the kitchen. I followed Alice around to the front where our bikes were.

'What's going on?' I asked. 'We don't need to bring food. Surely you don't think we're going to get lost on the way to the village?'

Before she could answer, Mum was back, with the stew all packed up in a bowl with a lid. She handed it to Alice, who strapped it on to the back of her bike.

'I'm so glad it's not going to waste,' said Mum.

Alice smiled at her.

'You can rely on me, Sheila,' she said. 'I promise not one single scrap will be wasted.'

I shook my head in wonder. Had Alice spent so long with our family that she was actually losing her mind?

Anyway, I had no time to wonder, as Alice was already half way up the road.

'Bye, Mum,' I called as I jumped on my bike. 'We'll be back in an hour. We promise. And this time we mean it.'

* * *

We got to Bruno's house, and Alice knocked on the door. Bruno answered. He was wearing denim shorts and a nice white t-shirt.

'Hey. Cool clothes,' said Alice, and Bruno smiled shyly.

'Is Pascal around?' asked Alice then.

'You want see Pascal?' asked Bruno.

Alice nodded.

'But ...' Bruno said.

'But ...' I said too.

Alice ignored us.

'I only want to see him for one minute,' she said. 'There's something I need to show him.'

Bruno looked at me.

I shrugged. How was I supposed to know what she was on about? She's only been my best friend for thirteen years.

'Whatever,' said Bruno, and I smiled. That was one of the words I'd taught him.

Bruno went inside and a few minutes later he was back with Pascal following a few steps behind him.

Pascal was fixing his hair as usual.

'What you want show me?' he said to Alice.

Alice smiled at him.

'It's over here,' she said, propping her bike against the garden wall. 'It's a surprise.'

Pascal walked towards her. As he passed Bruno, he gave him a sneering smile, as if to say, *See, I'm the cool one. I'm getting to see the surprise.*

Pascal stood beside Alice with his arms folded.

'What is surprise?' he said impatiently.

Alice unstrapped the bowl of lentil stew from the back of her bike.

'It's called lentil stew,' she said. 'It's an Irish delicacy.'

We all watched as she took the lid off the bowl, and held it towards Pascal. He looked in, sniffed, and said,

'I not like.'

I smiled. I agreed with him about that.

Then, before anyone could move, Alice gave a big laugh.

'You not like?' she said. 'Tough luck.'

Then in one quick movement, she lifted the bowl, flicked her wrist, and dumped the entire gooey, disgusting stew all over Pascal. It dripped down his precious hair, onto his face, and down on to his white t-shirt.

'Ooops,' said Alice happily. 'Sorry about that. My hand slipped.'

Pascal didn't say anything. Maybe he was afraid that if he opened his mouth, some of the stew might get in. He tried to wipe the stew off his face, but there was too much of it. The more he wiped, the messier it got. So in the end he just stood there, with slimy stuff dripping off him, into little brown puddles at his feet. He looked like an escapee from a horror movie.

I looked at Bruno. He was standing still with his mouth open, like he was in shock or something.

'It's funny,' I said. Then, suddenly he started to laugh, and as he laughed, Alice and I joined in.

'It very, *very* funny,' said Bruno, and we all laughed some more.

Pascal had had enough. He walked quickly in the side entrance of the bakery, slamming the door behind him.

Suddenly, there was a big screech from inside the bakery and Pascal came running out again, chased by a very cross-looking woman, who was shouting loudly in French.

'Is my mother!' said Bruno, 'She say Pascal make the floor not clean. He not happy! He has fear of my mother!'

Now Pascal was standing obediently in the garden, while Bruno's mother turned on a tap, and picked up a hose.

'She wouldn't!' gasped Alice, just as Bruno's mother turned the hose on Pascal.

Pascal screamed, but by now Bruno's mother was holding him tightly by one arm and he couldn't escape. He stood there shivering as every last drop of lentil stew was washed off him onto the ground. As soon as he was released, Pascal shook himself like a wet dog, and then ran inside again.

As soon as the rest of us had finished

laughing, I turned to Bruno.

'I hope he won't give you a hard time over this,'
I said.

Bruno laughed.

'It not matter. Is worth it. Anyway, he leave
tomorrow. Now you please wait here and I get
something.'

He ran into the bakery and returned with a bag
of pastries. The three of us sat in the square
eating them. Bruno wanted to hear all about our
night in the forest. Alice talked most, and listening to her, it sounded like a fun adventure,
instead of the totally scary experience it had
really been.

After a while Alice got up.

'I want to see the church one more time,' she
said.

Since when had Alice been so interested in
churches? I went to stand up, but she pushed me
down again.

'You wait here,' she said. 'I'll be back in three

minutes.'

Suddenly I knew that she wanted to leave me on my own with Bruno. As she walked away, I wondered desperately what I should say to him.

Sorry for thinking you were a loser?

Sorry for laughing at your shorts?

Sorry for using you just because we wanted to get close to Pascal?

Nothing sounded right, so I just said 'sorry about before', and Bruno didn't even ask why I was apologising. He just said 'is OK' and that seemed to be enough.

By then Alice was back.

We'd better go,' she said. 'Can't get your mum and dad worried again, can we?'

Bruno and I stood up. And we all walked over to where our bikes were propped against the wall of the bakery.

Bruno turned to Alice.

'*Au revoir*,' he said, and he kissed her on both cheeks, the way the French do.

Then he turned to me.

'*Au revoir*,' he said, and he kissed me too – first one cheek, and then the other. And then my tummy started to do funny, jumpy things, and I could feel my face going red.

Bruno went inside, and Alice turned to me.

'You like him,' she said. 'You really like him. Why didn't you tell me?'

I was going to deny it, but then changed my mind. After all, Alice and I had been through a lot together, so it wasn't right to have secrets from each other. I sighed.

'I didn't tell you before, because I didn't know until right this second.'

Alice laughed.

'That is sooo cool. Call him back, or run after him or something.'

I shook my head.

'We have to go. Mum will be going crazy. Looks like I left it a bit too late.'

Alice thought for a minute.

'When we get home, will I pretend my ankle is really sore, and your mum and dad will have to get a doctor for me, and then you'd have time to race back here to say a proper good-bye to Bruno?'

What was she like? I could see that Alice was perfectly serious.

I shook my head.'

'Thanks, Al, but no thanks. I think I've had more than enough excitement for this holiday.

Alice sighed.

'Whatever.'

Chapter Thirty-Three

When we got back to the house, Mum was waiting for us.

Alice handed her the empty bowl from the stew.

Mum smiled at her.

'Well, how was the stew?'

Alice beamed back at her.

'It was perfect. Just perfect,' she said, and Mum looked so happy I thought she was going to cry.

As soon as she recovered. Mum pulled us inside.

'Girls, come in and see what we bought for Lucy to say thank you for lending us the house,' she said.

We followed her inside, and Mum held up a huge painting.

'What do you think?' she said. 'Don't you think Lucy will love it?'

It was like my worst nightmare. It was a picture of a table covered with a big heap of vegetables.

'Er ... It's ... lovely,' I said.

'Lucky Lucy,' said Alice.

Mum seemed happy with that, so she went off in to the kitchen to hang the picture over the sink.

'It's bad enough Mum feeding us heaps of vegetables all the time,' I said. 'Without her buying pictures of them as well. I'm sorry, Alice, that my mum is so totally embarrassing.'

Alice looked at me.

'Megan,' she said. 'I think your mum is totally great.'

At first I thought she was joking.

'What about the crazy hair, and the crazy clothes, and the crazy ideas about chick peas and stuff?'

Alice laughed.

'That's only small stuff. Trust me, Meg, she's great. You're lucky to have a mum like her.'

And all of a sudden, I realised that she was right.

*   *   *

Twenty minutes later, we were all packed up and ready to leave. Just as Mum was locking the front door of Lucy's house for the last time, Alice's phone beeped. She looked at the screen.

'It's a text message from Grace,' she said, as she pressed the buttons. Then she read aloud,

'Hi Al and Meg. Lanzarote wasn't much fun this year. Hope your holiday wasn't too boring.'

Alice looked at me, and I looked at her, and

then we laughed until the tears streamed down our faces.

Then we all climbed in to the car, and set off for home.

THE 'ALICE & MEGAN' SERIES
BY
JUDI CURTIN

<u>HAVE YOU READ THEM ALL?</u>

Don't miss the other great books about
Alice & Megan:

Alice Next Door
Alice Again
Don't Ask Alice
Alice in the Middle
Alice & Megan Forever
Alice to the Rescue
Viva Alice!
Alice & Megan's Cookbook

Available from all good bookshops

www.obrien.ie

**VISIT
WWW.ALICEANDMEGAN.COM**